SOFIA'S CHOICE

LAURA HOLT-HASLAM

River Pony Press

2024

In memory of Robyn Cuffey (1954-2023)
Gifted artist, author, riding instructor, horse trainer, and
friend who loved riding and driving along the carriage trails of
Acadia National Park.

Chapter 1

Bright sunshine poured through the windows of Good Shepherd Community Church, warming the right side of Sofia's face. Her eyelids drooped, but she forced her eyes open, hoping Pastor Amy wouldn't notice her drowsiness.

Sofia and her friends Olivia and Ryan were in middle school, so they were expected to stay in the sanctuary for the entire worship service, including the sermon. Pastor Amy's booming voice and energetic movements usually held Sofia's attention, but she'd found it difficult to sleep last night, and she'd left the house before sunrise. The horses had to be fed, and the stalls mucked out whether or not she was sleepy.

Ryan jiggled his legs, causing the pew to vibrate with his twitchy energy. Olivia glared and tapped his foot with the bottom of her crutch. Sofia glanced up at their mother, Pastor Amy, wondering if she ever scolded her twins for their behavior during the worship service. If she did, Sofia hadn't witnessed it.

She looked across the aisle to her great-grandfather. Grampy's eyes were closed. He was either praying or napping. She suspected it was the latter.

Pastor Amy grinned at the congregation, most of whom still appeared to be awake. She invited them to pray with her, which meant her sermon was ending and they'd be singing one last song before they could go downstairs and socialize. Sofia hoped Grampy would hold off on his snoring for another minute or two.

At Pastor Amy's invitation, Sofia rose to her feet to join the church members in song. She struggled to follow the unfamiliar tune, hating the sound of her high, wispy voice. Thankfully, Olivia belted the words, drowning out everyone within a twenty-foot radius.

When the worship service was over, Olivia grabbed Sofia's arm. "Mrs. Smith made peanut butter cookies for the coffee hour. We better hurry downstairs and get our share before the Sunday School kids take them all."

"I'm on it." Ryan grinned before turning and sprinting down the side aisle ahead of the grownups.

"You'd better save some for us!" Olivia shouted at his back. It would take her three times as long as her brother to make it down the stairs and into the fellowship hall. She leaned on her crutches. "Aren't you coming?"

"I want to say hello to Mrs. Smith."

"Good luck with that," Olivia said, glancing at the line forming around the elderly woman. "I'll save you some cookies if Ryan doesn't eat them all before I get there."

Sofia nodded. Though her mouth watered at the thought of Mrs. Smith's peanut butter and chocolate kiss cookies, she wanted to check how Mrs. Smith was doing first. She'd only returned home from the nursing home a few days ago, and her cat, Pumpkin, was still living in Sofia's bedroom.

Mrs. Smith was speaking with a group of similarly elderly ladies when she spotted Sofia waiting for her turn to greet her. "Sofia," her voice rang out. "The angel who saved my life."

Sofia's cheeks grew warm, but she smiled as she approached Mrs. Smith. "I didn't save…"

"You most certainly did. If you hadn't found me on the floor and called for help, I'd be with Jesus in the sweet hereafter instead of in church with you and these lovely ladies." Mrs. Smith threw her arms around Sofia and kissed the top of her head. "Mmm. Your hair smells of horses."

"Sorry." Sofia stepped away from Mrs. Smith's embrace. "I didn't have time to take a shower this morning."

Mrs. Smith laughed. "You and I both know horse smell is the best aroma in the world. How is that lovely palomino of yours?"

"Sundance is doing great. And Anika is giving me a jumping lesson tomorrow."

"Ah. Your new horse-crazy friend." Mrs. Smith grinned. "Don't do anything I wouldn't do."

"Like jumping over picnic tables? Or cars?" Sofia giggled. She still had a difficult time imagining the elderly Mrs. Smith as a reckless teenager jumping her horse, Patches, over everything in sight. "I think we're going to practice with cross rails. Boring, I know."

"Remember, baby steps." Mrs. Smith put her arm around Sofia's shoulder. "I know a wise, young horse trainer who has had splendid success with this method."

Wise, young horse trainer. Sofia's chest warmed at Mrs. Smith's compliment. The barn owner, Stephanie, had taught her about taking baby steps, but it had been Sofia's patience and persistence that had helped Sundance to regain his confidence.

"I made your favorite cookies," Mrs. Smith said. "You'd better get one before they're gobbled up."

"Thanks."

Sofia hurried down the stairs to the fellowship room and tried to push past a group of elementary-age kids who crowded around the snack table. A plate containing fragments of crackers and three slices of cheese sat beside a bare platter. Mrs. Smith's cookies were gone.

Ryan tapped Sofia's shoulder and whispered, "Come with me."

She turned and followed him into Pastor Amy's office. Olivia sat behind her mother's desk, holding a paper plate with several peanut butter and chocolate kiss cookies.

"I can't believe you..." Sofia glanced at Ryan. "How many did you take?"

Ryan grinned. "Our fair share."

Olivia offered the plate of cookies to Sofia. "Three for each of us. Ryan already ate his, but I was polite enough to wait for you."

"You swiped *nine* cookies?" Sofia shook her head at Ryan. That seemed a bit more than a *fair share.*

"Uh, ten, actually." Ryan wiped his mouth. "But Mrs. Smith made a lot. And if I hadn't taken them, the Sunday school kids would have."

Sofia bit into a cookie, feeling slightly guilty, but not guilty enough to return the others to the empty platter in the fellowship room.

"So," Olivia said through a mouthful. "You're going to ask Jess whether we can ride Magic and Rosie, right?"

Sofia held back an eye roll. Olivia had asked her this question at least a dozen times since she'd told her that Mom's boyfriend, Jason, had a sister who owned two horses. Jason had ridden Jess's Percheron-cross, Black Magic, on a trail ride with Sofia and her horse Sundance, but she hadn't met Jess, or her horse, Rosie, yet. "I already told you I would."

"Yeah, but since you're going to her house after church, I just wanted to make sure you don't forget."

This time Sofia really did roll her eyes. "There's no way I'm going to forget." How could she, with Olivia and Anika bugging her constantly?

"Are you going to eat your other cookies?" Ryan asked Olivia.

"You've already had four." Olivia narrowed her eyes and snatched a cookie from the plate. She crammed it into her mouth. "If you keep eating like that, you'll get too fat to ride."

Ryan frowned and patted his stomach. "Maybe I don't care about riding."

"You're just a big, fat chicken." Olivia smirked. "Bok. Bok. Bok..."

Sofia glared at Olivia. Why did she have to be so mean to her brother? He'd fallen from Sundance less than two months ago. He'd even missed the first few days of school while he recovered from hitting his head. Sofia didn't blame him for being afraid to get back on a horse. She held out the plate of Mrs. Smith's cookies. "You can have one of mine."

Ryan shook his head and walked away.

Sofia's heart pounded as she considered confronting Olivia. How many times had she ignored her friend's hurtful comments to Ryan? Fifty times? A hundred? More? Ryan was Sofia's friend, too. She put the paper plate back on Pastor Amy's desk. "Why do you do that to him?"

"Do what?" Olivia took another bite of her cookie.

"Say mean things to him. Make him feel bad."

Olivia shrugged. "He's my brother. That's what sisters do. He knows I'm just teasing him."

Sofia took a deep breath before responding. "I'm not sure he always sees it that way. I think you hurt his feelings sometimes."

"What? About being a chicken?" Olivia jutted her chin. "He's gotta toughen up. Get back on a horse. The sooner he does that, the sooner he'll conquer his fears. Which is why you need to ask Jess if he can ride Magic. You said that horse is bombproof. Exactly the horse Ryan needs. And I can ride Rosie."

Sofia sighed. "I'll ask."

Mom jumped to her feet when Sofia and Grampy walked through the door. "You're late."

"Humph." Grampy's bushy, white mustache fluttered. "It's the same time we always get home from church. Which you'd know if you didn't sleep in every Sunday morning."

Sofia held back a grin. Mom was usually in her pajamas when they returned, but today she wore a form-fitting black dress, heels, and makeup. She'd swept her long, blonde hair into a fancy updo Sofia had seen movie actresses wear, but didn't know what was called. Olivia probably would. Sofia usually wore her thick, tightly curled dark hair in a ponytail, and when it was especially unruly, she topped it off with a baseball cap. Horses didn't care what her hair looked like.

But Mom did.

"Honey Bear." Mom sniffed. "You didn't take a shower after mucking out the stalls?"

"I didn't have time before church."

Mom groaned. "But you knew we were going to Jason's house afterward. You can't go smelling like a barn."

"But we're going to visit Jess's animals," Sofia protested. "What's the point in showering and getting all dressed up if we're going to walk through Jess's barn?"

Grampy chuckled.

"You stay out if it," Mom said.

Grampy raised his hands in mock surrender before picking up the newspaper and settling down in his favorite chair.

"Don't get too comfortable. We need to leave in a few minutes." Mom sighed. "I just want you to look nice. And smell nice. Jason's been working hard all morning in the kitchen, and wants to impress you and Grampy."

Grampy looked up from the paper. "He's already impressed me with the seafood paella he made us a couple of weeks ago. What is he cooking today?"

"He says it's a surprise."

"Hopefully Sofia didn't ruin her appetite at church, eating all of Mrs. Smith's cookies." Grampy laughed.

Sofia's eyes widened. How did Grampy find out?

"Honey Bear, please tell me you didn't." Mom shook her head.

"I...uh..." Sofia glanced at Grampy, who winked at her. "I better take a quick shower."

Chapter 2

S ofia tugged at her wet ponytail. It smelled of lavender shampoo, the same kind Gramma Lisa used. If she had to wash off the horsey scent, she might as well be reminded of her grandmother. She hadn't seen Gramma Lisa since the middle of August when she'd dropped off Sundance. They'd talked on the phone a few times since then, but Sofia missed her and her Morgan mare, Delilah.

"Can't we take Grampy's Subaru?" Sofia pleaded when Mom jingled the keys to her new-to-her vehicle, which Sofia and Grampy secretly referred to as the Rusty Rocket. Mom had purchased the old relic from her coworker at Ray's Variety a few days earlier. Sofia knew nothing about cars, but Grampy explained to her that at one time, in the *very* distant past, the faded red Mazda had been a speed demon, tearing up the road with youthful exuberance. Now, however, the once-proud engine wheezed and sputtered as if burdened by the weight of memories from its glory days. Sofia doubted whether it would make it through the winter.

"Stop complaining and get in," Mom said. "I don't want to be late."

The Rusty Rocket bounced over a pothole as they turned left onto a narrow road. They drove past the stubbly remains of a cornfield, the crop long since harvested and the stalks chopped down. The engine strained as the car struggled up a steep incline.

Grampy drummed his fingers against the dashboard, as if urging an exhausted racehorse to make it over the finish line. He let out an audible breath when they finally crested the hill.

"Jason lives way out in the middle of nowhere," Sofia said as they passed a field dotted with black and white cows.

"It's only fifteen minutes from town." Mom glanced at her through the cracked rear-view mirror. "And we're almost there."

Town. Sofia smiled. Two months ago, Mom had complained about moving to a small Maine town. She'd called the residents *country bumpkins.* If Grampy's house was in the country, Jason's must be out in the sticks. Not that Sofia minded. Jason said he lived near miles and miles of trails. Trails where he and his sister rode Magic and Rosie. Trails where *she* could ride Sundance.

"He lives there." Mom pointed ahead and to the left at a tan ranch-style house.

So, Jess must live across... "Hey, I see Magic!" Sofia craned her neck to the right as they passed a pasture and an old barn at the bottom of a hill. The huge, black Percheron-cross nibbled grass beside a smaller Appaloosa who must be Rosie.

Mom pulled into Jason's short driveway. She'd barely turned off the sputtering engine when a woof, followed by a string of high-pitched barks, sounded from the backyard. A moment later, two dogs barreled down the driveway.

"Einstein! Harriet!" A woman's voice called after them.

A yellowish colored dog—some sort of lab mix?—slowed at the sound of her voice, but the smaller one bounded forward, leaping at the car.

"Harriet, get back here!" the woman yelled.

The side door of Jason's house flew open, and Mom's boyfriend ran down the steps. "Come on, you silly dog."

Harriet yipped and jumped at the car again.

Jason grinned at them before scooping the squirming dog into his arms. "It's safe to come out. She's just excited. All bark and no bite."

Sofia hurried out of the Rusty Rocket and ran to Jason. "She's adorable! I love Boston Terriers." She rubbed her hand over the dog's pointy, black ears and giggled at her bulging eyes and flat face.

The yellow dog trotted toward Jason and Sofia, his wagging tail causing his entire body to shimmy with excitement. A red-headed woman jogged after him. "Come here, Einstein."

Einstein ignored her command and bumped his nose against Sofia's leg. "Don't be jealous. You're cute, too." She bent to pet him.

"Sorry about my dogs," the young woman said, holding out her hand. "I'm Jess."

"Nice to meet you." Sofia was about to shake hands with Jason's sister when she realized her own hand was covered with dog drool. She wiped it on the tan pants Mom had insisted she wear instead of her usual jeans. Thankfully, Mom, who was stepping out of her car, didn't appear to have noticed. Sofia glanced at her leg. At least it didn't leave a green stain, like Sundance's slobber would have.

"Hey, Babe. You look gorgeous." Jason approached Mom, grinning. Harriet still wriggled against his chest. "Want a doggie kiss?"

Mom stepped back. "I'm good, thanks."

Jess smiled at Mom. "Hi, Mandi. I'm so glad you could bring Sofia and your grandfather. Mr. Richardson?"

Grampy nodded. "You can call me Bill."

"Bill. Thanks so much for coming." Jess brushed dirt from the front of her bright orange fleece jacket. "Jason's been busy working in the kitchen. I was just out back, stacking some wood. I didn't realize this was a dressy sort of affair."

"Even if it was, you wouldn't be caught dead in a dress." Jason barked out a laugh before releasing Harriet, who jumped up against Sofia's leg, leaving a streak of mud. She couldn't help noticing that Jason wore a plaid flannel shirt and jeans with a hole in the left knee. Hardly dress-up clothes.

"You really do look amazing," Jason said to Mom. He wrapped his arms around her waist and kissed her on the lips. "I'll change into something nicer before we eat. But first, Sofia and Mr. Richardson need the grand tour."

"You really can call me Bill," Grampy said.

"Yes, sir, Mr. Richardson."

Grampy chuckled. "Fine. Call me anything you like, as long as you don't call me late for dinner."

"Good one, Mr. Richardson." Jason reached for Mom's hand. "Come on inside. The meal isn't ready yet, but I've put some appetizers on the table. Just don't let Jess's dogs inside, or they'll gobble them up before you have a chance to try one."

"Just like Mrs. Smith's cookies." Grampy fixed his gaze on Sofia.

"I only ate three," she muttered.

While similar in size and layout to Grampy's house, the inside of Jason's appeared more spacious and much less cluttered. Jason's floors were hardwood rather than wall-to-wall carpet. And unlike the mismatched old furniture at Grampy's, Jason's living room had a couch and two armchairs covered in the same creamy-white fabric. A large television was mounted on the wall.

"Help yourself." Jason pointed to a fruit platter on the coffee table. "I'll be right out with the shrimp tarts."

Sofia speared a strawberry with a toothpick and popped it into her mouth. Weren't tarts something you ate for dessert? Why put shrimp on them?

Jason returned, carrying the plate of shrimp tarts. Jess snatched one before he put it on the table. "These are the best," she said, and crammed the entire thing into her mouth.

"Try one, Sofia," Jason urged. "Before Jess eats them all."

Sofia examined the pastry shell and the pink shrimp tail poking out from the top. "What's the stuff inside?"

"Cream cheese and cocktail sauce. Puts hair on your chest." Jason grinned.

Sofia rolled her eyes, but couldn't help smiling at Jason's now familiar teasing. The first time he'd told her this, he'd been referring to Moxie, the most disgusting soda she'd ever tasted. "As long as it tastes as good as your seafood paella."

"Even better. I promise."

"Mmm, he's right." Grampy licked his fingers.

"Jason's a brilliant chef." Mom reached for a tart. "I don't know why he doesn't do this professionally."

Sofia took a tentative bite. The pastry flaked on her tongue. It *was* good. She grabbed a second one.

Jess helped herself to two more shrimp tarts. "Hey, Jason, how much longer before dinner's ready?"

"I think it will be another half hour," he called from the kitchen.

"Want to make a quick trip to my place and see the menagerie?" Jess asked.

Sofia wasn't sure what a menagerie was, but if it had anything to do with Magic and Rosie... She jumped up from her chair. "I want to come."

"I'd love to see the animals," Grampy said.

Mom smoothed her dress and glanced at her high heels. "I'll stay here and keep Jason company."

Chapter 3

Einstein and Harriet danced around Sofia's legs as she and Grampy followed Jess across the road. Jess's long driveway sloped downhill, with a strip of electric fence winding along to the right of it. From the other side of the fence, Magic and Rosie nibbled on the sparse, patchy grass.

Grazing next to sixteen-two hand, draft-sized Magic, Rosie looked more like a large pony than a horse, though Sofia realized she must be around the size of Sundance, about fifteen hands. The red roan Appaloosa looked up from the grass. White hairs frosted her rump. The rest of her coat was an almost equal mixture of white and chestnut-colored hairs, though her legs were more solidly chestnut. She swished her thin, reddish tail.

Jess whistled. Magic's head shot up, and his ears pricked forward between his thick forelock. He stared at Jess and the others, unblinking, while Rosie appeared to ignore them.

When Jess reached into her pocket, however, Rosie nickered and trotted toward the fence. The mare eagerly gobbled the horse treat from her outstretched hand.

Magic arrived a few moments later, his eyes fixed on Jess's pocket.

"Want to give him a cookie?" Jess handed the treat to Sofia.

"Sure." Sofia reached over the fence, careful not to brush her sleeve against the electrified wire. Magic's upper lip flapped against her palm.

The dogs circled Jess, who laughed and reached into her other pocket. "You two are such pigs."

The corners of Grampy's mouth twitched under his bushy mustache. "So, did you just happen to load your pockets with treats this afternoon?" he asked, "Or is this more of an everyday occurrence?"

"I like to be prepared." Jess chuckled as Harriet licked her fingers. "Jason thinks I spoil them too much. But then, he's the one putting on this dinner to impress you."

"He's already impressed me with his cooking," Grampy said. "And he's a nice young man. I'm so glad Mandi has—"

"Tell me about Rosie," Sofia interrupted. She knew it was rude, but a conversation about Mom and Jason's romantic relationship was the last thing she wanted to listen to. If Mom had to date someone, she was glad it was Jason and not Paul, or one of the other boyfriends she'd been with over the past few years, but thinking about him kissing Mom made her skin prickle.

"We call her the Sassy Appy." Jess scratched Rosie's neck. The mare leaned against Jess's hand and lifted her head. "She's not as sassy now as when I bought her, but she still likes to let us know she thinks she's in charge of this place. She even pushes Magic around."

"How long have you owned her?" Sofia asked.

"I got her as a two-year-old filly, just after Jason and I bought this place. So that must have been eight years ago, after I graduated from college. We were getting this big, old barn, and it wasn't right to keep Magic alone. Plus, I wanted Jason to ride with me. On Magic, that is, not on his ATV. I broke Rosie to saddle, like I did with Magic."

"You and Jason own this place together?" Grampy asked, sounding surprised.

"Yeah. Jason insisted I graduate from college, first, even though *he* didn't go. He was always telling me what to do." She laughed. "He still is. And he'll be mad at me if we don't get back when dinner's ready. Can I show you the rest of the animals?" Jess turned away from Rosie and headed down the driveway. The mare followed from the other side of the fence.

Sofia rubbed Magic's forehead before jogging after them. Mom couldn't afford a house, let alone two houses and a barn. Did this mean Jason and Jess were rich? Jason didn't drive a fancy car like Anika's mother, and he acted nothing like Mom's snobbish former fiancé, Paul. She couldn't think of a polite way to ask, so she settled on a different question.

"Jason says you have a miniature donkey?" Sofia hadn't seen one in the pasture.

"Tootsie." Jess continued walking without slowing her pace. "I keep her in a paddock behind the barn. I don't think Rosie and Magic would hurt her on purpose, but..."

"I get it," Sofia said. "There are two mini horses where I board Sundance. Stephanie keeps them separate from Sundance, too."

Jess nodded. "Snickers and Kit Kat. They're so adorable."

Sofia's eyes widened. "You've met them?"

"I saw them at horse shows a long time ago. Back when Stephanie's kids were showing. They must be grown up now."

"Grace is in college," Sofia said. "She's the leader of the Mini Whinnies. That's the horse club I'm in."

Jess whirled back to face Sofia. "No way! I remember the Mini Whinnies. Stephanie led it. And Grace was just a little kid in pigtails, but she won everything with Kit Kat. Every class! And now she leads the club and you're in it?"

"Kit Kat still wins everything. At least she did at the horse show we went to in August."

This was the perfect opening to ask the question her friends had been pestering her about for the past two weeks. It had seemed like a simple request, but as she followed Jess and Grampy down the hill toward the barn, Sofia's insides churned. Would she come across as demanding as Olivia and Anika? But if she didn't ask, they'd complain until she did.

Sofia took a deep breath. "Jason mentioned you might let my friends from the Mini Whinnies come over and ride sometime."

"He told me." Jess led them around the side of the barn. "He said you share your horse with them. Are they really your friends, or are they just using you? Because I know what it's like when you get a horse. All of a sudden people you barely know want to become your best friend just so they can get some free rides."

"No, it's not like that." Sofia felt like she'd just been punched in the gut. "They're my real friends." *At least, I think they are.*

Jess ran her fingers through her strawberry-blonde, shoulder-length hair. "I just wanted to be sure before I agreed. Maybe you can bring them after school this week. I get out of work early on Wednesdays. I should be home by three."

Anika and Olivia would be thrilled. Would Ryan? At least she knew he wasn't friends with her just because she had a horse.

Sofia and Grampy followed Jess to a fenced-in paddock about the size of Snickers and Kit Kat's. Tootsie's enormous, shaggy ears swiveled toward Jess. The donkey's nostrils flared. She opened her mouth and sucked in a breath, like she was yawning.

"Cover your ears," Jess warned.

Sofia and Grampy flinched when the tiny donkey brayed. Picture books and songs claimed donkeys said "heehaw", but the noise coming from Tootsie's gaping jaws sounded more like a trumpet blast mixed with a lion roaring and goose honking, punctuated by breathy squeaks. Just when Sofia thought Tootsie was finished, she brayed again.

"That's her way of saying hello," Jess said.

"Quite a greeting," Grampy said.

Tootsie swished her bristly tail and approached the fence. She was about the size of Snickers, though her neck was skinnier and her belly rounder.

"Are mini donkeys like mini horses?" Sofia asked. "Can you do the same things with them? Like drive or go over jumps?"

"Some people drive them, but mostly they're just cute pets. They're also great guard animals. If Tootsie sees anything out of the ordinary, she lets us know."

"I bet you can hear her all the way from Jason's house." Sofia chuckled.

Grampy gestured toward a pair of brown and tan floppy-eared goats at the far side of the paddock. "When are they expecting?"

"Never. They're boys." Jess laughed at the expression on Grampy's face. "But you're right. They look like they're about to give birth to twins. Or triplets. Billy the Kid and Vincent Van Goat are the fattest goats in the history of the world."

Grampy shook his head. "You're not kidding. They're wider than they are tall."

"Believe it or not, they're on a diet. They belong to our Great Aunt Betty, who spoiled them rotten. She's ninety-two and isn't able to take care of them anymore, so Jason and I took them under our wing in September."

"What's the other goat's name?" Sofia asked. The cinnamon-colored goat's ears stuck out from the sides of his head. He was shorter than the other two, stocky, but not pregnant looking.

"Weaselface. Weasel for short." Jess snorted. "Jason named him after my ex-boyfriend."

Sofia giggled, thinking Weaselface might be a good nickname for Mom's ex-fiancé, Paul.

"You and Jason are quite close," Grampy observed.

"We are." Jess scratched behind Tootsie's ear. "I don't know how much he's told you about what it was like growing up. Dad died when I was thirteen, and Mom... I'll just say it was hard for her to handle her grief. If it hadn't been for Jason, I don't know what would have happened to me. He's kind of like my dad, big brother, and best friend all rolled up into one person."

"He told me he took you to a lot of horse shows, but I didn't realize your father..." Sofia swallowed. Her own father had abandoned her when she was three and a half years old, but at least he hadn't died. She'd grown up knowing nothing about him or her Dominican-American family until a few months ago, when she'd received a birthday card from her grandmother, Abuela. A few weeks later, a second letter arrived from a woman named Daniella, claiming to be her stepmother. Daniella and Sofia's father were expecting a baby together. It was a lot to process.

Sofia pushed aside her conflicting thoughts about her father. "That must have been really hard."

Jess nodded. "But I had Jason, and he helped me to buy and take care of Black Magic. There's nothing like training a young horse to keep your mind occupied." She patted Tootsie's rump. "I haven't introduced you to the chickens, but I think we'd better get back to the house. We don't want to be late."

Jason greeted them at the top of the hill, wearing a bright yellow apron over a blue dress shirt and a red tie. He waved both arms, beckoning them forward. "Hurry, hurry. I don't want to serve you cold lasagna."

Grampy panted for breath and wiped his hand across his forehead.

"Oh, no! Mr. Richardson." Jason hurried to his side. "That's a steep climb. I should have driven you back in the truck."

Grampy shook his head. "Are you implying I'm too old to walk up a hill without assistance?"

Jason's cheeks flushed. "No, Mr. Richardson. Of course not."

Sofia glanced at Grampy, whose mustache twitched. "He's just teasing you, aren't you, Grampy."

Grampy made a humphing sound and crossed his arms. "I'll let it slide, seeing as you made dinner for us."

Jess laughed. "I definitely did not get the memo about this being a fancy affair. Can I take five minutes to change? I'll bring Harriet and Einstein home so they won't beg." Without waiting for an answer, Jess turned back down the hill. Einstein bounded after her, his thick, yellow tail wagging joyfully. Harriet's paws remained cemented to the ground.

Jason flicked his arm toward his sister's house. "Go on, you silly mutt."

The Boston Terrier looked up at Sofia with her bulging eyes. "I can take her back," Sofia said.

"She'll head home as soon as we go inside. The spinach lasagna awaits."

"Spinach?" Sofia's nose wrinkled.

"Puts hair on your chest." Jason winked.

"In that case," she said, "I'd better give it a try."

<h1 style="text-align:center">Chapter 4</h1>

S ofia's mouth watered as she took a second bite of the lasagna. The green stuff must be spinach, but the combination of herbs and cheeses hid the taste of it, or at least she thought it did, since she couldn't remember eating spinach before.

Jess sat beside her and across the table from Grampy. She'd pulled her hair back with a gold-colored barrette and was now wearing a rumpled green sundress. "Hey, Jason. Remember Allison? My friend from college?"

"The girl who owns that monster Thoroughbred? How could I forget her?" Jason rubbed his arm.

"Thor bit him," Jess explained, "though it served Jason right for hitting on Allison.

"I did not." Jason patted the top of Mom's hand. "I've only ever had eyes for this lovely lady."

Jess snorted in a most unladylike manner.

Jason's cheeks flushed nearly as red as his beard. "Okay, but that was before I met Mandi."

Sofia glanced at Mom's frowning face before pivoting her focus to the slice of homemade garlic bread resting on her plate. She'd rather not know what Mom might think about Allison or the other women Jason liked before meeting Mom. It wasn't as if she hadn't dated other men in the past.

"She called right as I was leaving my house," Jess continued, as if nothing had just happened. "Allison's cousin bought a boarding stable and lesson barn in Ellsworth. It's only twenty minutes from Acadia National Park. She doesn't have many clients yet, which means..." Jess leaned forward, her eyes bright. "We can take Rosie and Magic to Acadia again. And," she grinned at Sofia, whose head had popped up at the mention of *boarding stable*, "Sofia and Sundance could come, too."

Sofia sat straighter in her chair. "Really? You'd take us?"

Jess nodded. "She said there's room on her horse trailer for Sundance. Allison will take Thor, of course." She grinned at Jason, who scowled back.

"Acadia's beautiful," Grampy said to Sofia. "It's on an island, with the ocean and forests and mountains. Grammy and I used to hike there every summer. The park has miles and miles of carriage roads and trails."

"You should come, too, Mr. Richardson," Jason said. "We can make it a family thing."

Sofia's stomach fluttered. *A family thing.* Jason wasn't her father, and she'd only met Jess an hour ago. And yet, here they were, sitting around a table eating Sunday dinner together like a real family.

What were Abuela, Daddy, and his wife, Daniella doing now? Were they enjoying a meal with the aunts and uncles and cousins Sofia had never met? She thought of them eating and laughing together without her. They didn't know Sofia, except through a few pictures and letters exchanged over the past few weeks. She'd been invited to visit them over Christmas vacation, around the time her brother was supposed to be born. Would they feel like family or strangers?

"What horse do you want me to ride?" Grampy asked.

"I...uh..." Jason squirmed in his chair.

Grampy grinned. "You'd have to rent a fork-lift to get me on. I haven't ridden a horse since I was a kid, and I'm not about to pick it up again when I'm eighty. Mandi and I can keep our feet on the ground."

Mom looked away, her face pink.

Acadia National Park! Olivia and Anika would be so jealous.

"When are we going?" Sofia asked.

"Veteran's Day weekend. We'll leave Friday morning and come back Sunday afternoon, so that gives us a couple of hours to ride on Friday, all day Saturday, and a ride on Sunday morning. It will be chilly, and most of the fall foliage will be gone, but at least there won't be bugs or many tourists. Hopefully no snow, either."

"It snows in November?" Sofia rubbed her arms, remembering the winter barn chores at Gramma Lisa's house.

"Not usually that early. If it does, it will just be a few flakes." Jess folded her hands on the table beside her plate. "So, you're all coming? Jason can ride Magic, I'll ride Rosie, Sofia rides Sundance, and Bill and Mandi can...uh..."

Mom frowned. "Wait around doing nothing all weekend?"

Grampy wiped his mouth with his napkin. "You and I can see the sights together. Maybe get some popovers at Jordan Pond House if they're still open. Or visit Thunder Hole."

"And there are lots of shops in Bar Harbor," Jason added.

"Sure." Mom bit her lip. "Meanwhile, you and Allison can catch up. You can reminisce about old times."

"Allison?" Jason pulled back, looking like a scolded puppy. "You don't need to worry about her."

Sofia's gaze darted between Mom, Jason, and Jess before settling on Grampy, who sighed.

"Jess was just giving me a hard time, Mandi." Jason reached for Mom's hand again. "But if it would make you feel better, I won't ride with them. You and I can go sightseeing. Or shopping. Or whatever you want. We don't even have to go to Acadia with them at all, if you don't want to."

"But what about Grampy?" Sofia asked, annoyed that Mom's jealous outburst might ruin the chance of a family trip to Acadia.

Jason stroked the tops of Mom's fingers. She looked around the table, pouting.

Sofia held her breath.

"I've been to Acadia before," Grampy said before he sighed again. "I'm sure you don't want an old man getting in the way."

"Mr. Richardson, I didn't mean—"

"I'm sorry, Grampy," Mom said. "I want you to come. You can show Jason and me the places you and Grammy loved to hike. And the place you called the thunder something."

"Thunder Hole." Grampy said, a smile reappearing on his lined face. "If you go there when the tide is right...you're going to love it."

"A family trip to Acadia." Jason rubbed his hands together, grinning at Mandi. "But who is going to ride Magic? Maybe one of Sofia's friends can come along, too."

Sofia nearly jumped from her chair. "That would be great!"

But which friend?

Not Ryan. Even if he wasn't terrified of getting back on a horse, he'd only ridden a few times. He didn't know the basics of handling a horse in a riding ring, let alone a trail. Even Sofia had struggled to keep Sundance under control when she and Jason went on a trail ride together.

If Sofia invited Olivia, it wouldn't be fair to leave Ryan out, so she'd have to invite him, too. What would he do while they rode? Walk around with Grampy, Mom, and Jason? He'd be bored.

Anika was a much more experienced and confident rider than Ryan. Though Sofia didn't want to admit it, Anika might be a better rider than she was, at least with jumping. But they'd only been friends for a few weeks. If she chose Anika, Olivia would be angry and jealous.

Jess shook her head, frowning slightly. "I agree it would be fun for Sofia to bring a friend along. But I haven't met them, or their parents. Let's not get ahead of ourselves." Her face softened as she turned to Sofia. "I hope you understand. We're going to be in the saddle for several hours a day. I don't want anyone getting hurt. I need to meet your friends and watch them ride before I make any promises."

Sofia blew out a breath. She wouldn't have to choose between her friends.

Yet.

Chapter 5

Sundance leaned against Sofia's hand as she rubbed a curry comb over his muscular neck. The palomino Quarter Horse's lips twitched with pleasure.

"That feels good, doesn't it?" Sofia massaged harder, working it in circles over his back and rump. A cloud of dust rose from his hindquarters. She knocked the curry comb against the barn floor, leaving a small pile of dirt and short, yellow hairs. Sundance's summer coat was shedding out, replaced with the thicker, longer hair he'd need to keep him warm and dry during the winter.

Anika was late, as usual. Had Sofia missed a text from her?

When she checked her phone, Sundance nudged her shoulder. "Just give me a second, silly," she said as she stepped sideways.

No missed call or text.

Anika would probably show up after Sofia had finished all the chores, insisting it wasn't her fault. She claimed her mother arrived at least a half hour late for everything except her stepbrother's soccer games. Noah got all the attention, Anika complained, while she received all the nagging. At least her mother had finally relented and allowed her to ride Sundance, but only if there was an adult riding instructor present. Of course, there weren't any riding instructors at Stephanie's barn, so Anika still couldn't ride, not that it had stopped her from hopping on Sundance when her mom wasn't around to witness it.

Sofia sighed and returned the phone to her pocket. When she finished grooming Sundance, she grabbed the broom and dustpan from their hooks on the wall and tidied up. Stephanie appreciated a clean barn, and daily chores were part of the arrangement for Sundance's board.

Grampy wandered through the open barn door. "Your friend is still not here."

Sofia rolled her eyes and shook her head at Grampy's observation.

"How's Mr. Sundance today?" Grampy tickled Sundance's muzzle. The gelding's lips explored his fingers.

"Grampy, you're teasing him. He thinks you're giving him a treat."

"Good thing I brought this, then." Grampy pulled a piece of carrot from his coat pocket and offered it to Sundance. "I learned that trick from Jess. So, have you decided who you want to bring to Acadia if she approves?"

"No. And I haven't mentioned it to my friends yet, so please don't say anything."

"My lips are sealed." Grampy flicked his fingers over his bushy mustache.

Sofia was tightening Sundance's girth when Anika burst into the barn, her long black hair swishing behind her. "I'm sorry I'm late. Mum is so annoying... Oh, hello Mr. Richardson." She smiled at Grampy before kissing Sundance on the nose. "Ready for your jumping lesson?"

Sofia's pulse quickened. This would be her third time jumping with Anika's guidance. They'd started with poles on the ground and had progressed to low cross rails, but Anika had already jumped Sundance over a two and a half foot vertical, proclaiming Sundance a natural. She hadn't said the same about Sofia.

Without waiting for an answer, Anika retrieved Sundance's bridle, lifted the reins over his neck and unclipped the cross ties. "Why don't you put your helmet on while I get him ready?"

"What do you mean 'while I get him ready'?" Sofia struggled to keep her growing irritation from creeping into her voice. "I'm the one who cleaned three stalls and groomed my dirty horse while I waited for you to show up."

"I said I was sorry. It's Mum's fault I was late." Anika eased the snaffle bit into Sundance's mouth. "I can't wait until I meet Rosie and Magic. I'm sure Jess will let me ride them."

Sofia buckled the throat strap on her helmet, hoping Grampy would keep his promise not to mention Acadia. "Jess wants to meet you and Ryan and Olivia before she agrees to let you ride."

"But you told her I was an advanced rider, right?" Anika adjusted Sundance's noseband. "Did you let her know I'm teaching you how to jump?"

"She knows you and Olivia are good riders."

"I don't know about Olivia. I mean, she's..." Anika shrugged.

Sofia narrowed her eyes. "She's been riding since she was four. Which is longer than either of us."

"I'm not trying to put her down or anything. But we both know it's not the same."

"Why not?" Sofia snapped.

Anika raised her hands, startling Sundance.

Sofia's throat burned. Anika was only saying out loud what Sofia had often thought secretly. Olivia was different. She knew more about horses than any other person Sofia knew, but Olivia's disability was hard to ignore. "Sorry I got kind of..." Sofia wasn't sure what to say.

"I get it. She's your friend."

"She's your friend, too."

"I guess." Anika handed the reins to Sofia. "So, let's see you and Sundance jump some fences."

Sofia led Sundance from the barn to the minis' paddock, which doubled as their riding ring. What did Anika mean by 'I guess'? They were the Mini Whinnies! Anika seemed to be closer to Ryan than Olivia, but she was always friendly to both of them. Or was she?

Olivia had eaten lunch at Anika's table a few times, but the other girls had ignored her. This annoyed Olivia so much she'd stopped sitting with them, returning to Ryan's table in the corner of the lunchroom.

Anika opened the paddock gate and called to the miniature horse, Snickers. The blue-eyed bay pinto strode to her side and sniffed at her pockets. "Hey cutie. You aren't allowed to have treats, but Sofia left some yummy hay in your stall." She haltered him, then approached Kit Kat.

"I can take him for you," Grampy offered.

"They're little. I can handle both horses at the same time."

Sofia looked at Grampy, hoping he'd tell Anika not to do it. Grace sometimes led both minis at once, but she was their owner. What would happen if one of them spooked, or they got tangled up with each other while Anika led them into the barn?

"I need a job," Grampy said. "Please let me take Snickers. I don't want to stand around feeling useless."

"Okay." Anika smiled and gave Snickers' lead rope to Grampy.

Sofia let out a breath, silently thanking her great-grandfather for intervening. Maybe having adult supervision wasn't such a bad thing, after all.

While Grampy and Anika brought the minis into the barn, Sofia checked that Sundance's girth was tight and pulled down her stirrup irons. Since she'd be jumping, she shortened the leathers by one hole from their usual position. She mounted Sundance before Anika and Grampy returned to the paddock.

"After you get warmed up, we can start with trotting poles." Anika inspected Sofia and Sundance as if she were a professional riding instructor rather than her sixth-grade classmate.

The irritation Sofia had tried to suppress prickled over her skin. Sundance stiffened, feeling the tension in her body. *Relax.* She blew out a long breath.

They walked along the fence, circled, and changed directions. Sundance lowered his head. She squeezed her calves against his sides, moving him into a trot.

"Heels down," Anika called out.

Sofia clenched her jaw even as she pushed her weight down into her heels.

"I'm going to set out some trotting poles. You can practice your jumping position as you go over them." Anika rolled three wooden poles into the middle of the ring. She measured the distance between them using her footprints, readjusting them several times. "See if this works."

Sofia circled around the paddock again, partly to prepare for the correct approach over the trotting poles, but also to show Anika she could make her own decisions. She raised her head and pushed her heels down. Sundance lengthened his stride and lifted his knees as he trotted over the poles.

"You look great, Sofia," Grampy said from the other side of the fence.

Anika added a fourth pole. "Why don't you try this from the other direction?"

After they'd trotted over poles for several minutes, Anika dragged the wooden jumping standards from the far side of the paddock. "Cross rail time!" She moved a trotting pole to the jump, positioning one end in the cup and the other on the ground beside the opposite jumping standard. She placed the second pole to form an x shaped jump.

The center of the cross rail was only about six inches from the ground—hardly an impressive jump—but Sofia's heart raced. Most horses would only trot over it, but Sundance loved to jump. She grabbed a handful of his mane as they approached.

"Relax. Breathe." Anika said.

Why would Sofia need to be reminded to breathe? Everyone breathed unless they were dead.

Oh.

She hadn't realized she'd been holding her breath. She wondered how Anika could have known.

Sundance trotted toward the little jump. His hindquarters bunched underneath him, and he sprang forward. The momentum pushed Sofia's chest close to her horse's neck, but a second later, her body lurched backward. Her left foot fell out of her stirrup.

"He's such a good boy," Anika said. "He doesn't take advantage of you like a lot of lesson horses would."

Sofia kicked her foot back into the stirrup and patted Sundance's neck. He was a good boy. But she'd also done a lot of work training him and helping him to feel more confident. Work Anika knew nothing about.

Refusing to wait for another one of Anika's wannabe riding teacher commands, she squeezed Sundance back into a trot and approached the cross rail again. This time, she was prepared for Sundance's landing. She kept her feet in both stirrups while remaining in the correct jumping position the entire time.

"That was a lot better," Anika said. "Want to try a higher cross rail? I can just put it up a peg on each side."

"I want us to jump this one again first. Then we can move it up." Sofia wasn't sure what compelled her to push against Anika's instructions. Her friend was a lot more experienced in jumping than she was, and Anika was only trying to help.

After Sofia and Sundance jumped the low cross rail again, Anika raised the height. The middle part of the jump wasn't much taller than it had been before, but because the sides were higher, forming steeper angles, it looked a lot bigger. Sofia took two deep breaths to calm her nerves before circling back toward the jump. Sundance pricked his ears and trotted eagerly forward. She pushed her heels down, positioned herself over the saddle, and grabbed a handful of mane, just in case. If she lost her balance again, she didn't want to jerk on Sundance's mouth.

They leaped over and landed safely on the other side. Sofia grinned.

"Great," Anika said. "Want to try it in a canter?"

Sofia signaled Sundance, and a moment later, they were cantering around the paddock. As they approached the cross rail, Sundance's strides quickened. Sofia eased back on the reins to prevent her horse from galloping, though maybe they already were. He leaped from the ground, Sofia clinging to his mane. She nearly lost her stirrups when they landed, but she regained her balance quickly.

"Wow!" Anika shouted. "He flew over that. You might want to slow him down a bit next time."

"I tried to," Sofia panted, struggling to bring Sundance back to the trot. "He gets so excited to jump."

"You're so lucky. He's going to win you a lot of blue ribbons. You'll show him next summer, right?"

"If I can find someone to bring me." Trotting now, Sofia changed directions.

"Maybe Stephanie or Grace can take us. We can make it a Mini Whinnies thing. Or Jess can go with us. We can bring Rosie and Magic. I'll ask her on Wednesday."

Sofia shook her head.

"What?" Anika asked.

"Nothing."

Sofia jumped Sundance over the bigger cross rail four more times before telling Anika that it was probably enough for one day.

Anika ran her fingers through her long hair. "Can I get on him? Take a few fences?"

"But didn't your mother say you couldn't unless there was a riding instructor around?" Sofia glanced at Grampy, who hardly qualified as an experienced equestrian.

Anika pouted, but said nothing. She probably didn't dare to push it further with Grampy there as a witness.

Sofia gave Sundance a loose rein. He lowered his head and snorted out a contented sigh. "We could lead Snickers and Kit Kat over some jumps. Your mother's okay with that."

"It's better than nothing." Anika gave Sundance's neck a pat. "Actually, that would be fun. I want to show with Kit Kat next summer, too."

"If Olivia will let you," Sofia said.

Anika shrugged. "We can take turns. Plus, we'll have lots of classes to choose from with two minis and three riding horses."

"If Jess lets us bring Magic and Rosie."

"She will."

Sofia closed her eyes and tried not to think about what would happen when Anika found out about the trip to Acadia.

Chapter 6

After untacking Sundance and leading him back to his pasture, Sofia and Anika groomed the minis. Anika claimed dibs on Kit Kat, as she was the superior jumper, but Sofia didn't mind. As perfect as the tiny chestnut mare was, Snickers would always be Sofia's favorite.

Anika ran a soft brush down Kit Kat's crooked white blaze. "I'm turning twelve next week. On October 30."

"Happy birthday." Sofia picked up Snickers' hoof. It was packed with manure, as usual. "Is it weird to have a birthday so close to Halloween?"

"Not weird, but annoying sometimes. Who wants spiders and bats for their birthday party decorations? Or black and orange, when your favorite colors are pink and purple?" Anika playfully tousled Kit Kat's forelock. "Maybe it's kind of babyish to have a birthday party when you're twelve, but Mum's letting me invite a bunch of friends over. So, are you coming?"

"Really? I'm invited?"

"Of course. It's on Saturday night at my house."

"And Ryan and Olivia?"

Anika hesitated.

"Aren't they invited, too?"

"I didn't..." Anika shifted from foot to foot. "Don't take it the wrong way or anything. I just didn't know if they'd feel comfortable. You know, fit in."

The prickly sensation Sofia had experienced earlier returned. "But we're the Mini Whinnies Horse Club," she said, trying not to sound as irritated as she felt.

"This isn't a Mini Whinnies thing."

Sofia bit her lip. After Anika stood up for Ryan at school a few weeks before, James, Emily, and a few other kids had stopped talking to her for a few days. James still avoided Anika, shooting her dirty looks in class and hallways. Was she still afraid of losing her popularity?

Anika rested her hand on Kit Kat's back. "I guess that sounds wrong, doesn't it?"

"It's your party, but..." Sofia blew out a long breath.

Anika nodded. "It wouldn't be fair to leave them out. They can come, too."

The sun had slipped below the horizon by the time Sofia and Grampy returned home. Grampy was sorting through the day's mail when he held out a letter addressed to Sofia. "It looks like you have another letter from your father."

No longer worried about hiding her contact with Abuela, Daddy, and his wife, Daniella, Sofia had gotten out of the habit of racing to the mailbox the moment she got home from school. She snatched the letter from Grampy's hand. The handwriting on the envelope was definitely her father's. Inside was a brief note and a fuzzy black-and-white photo.

"It's another sonogram picture of my brother." She studied the blurry outline of what must be Santiago's head, then read Daddy's note.

Dear Sofia,

How are you? And how is your magnificent horse?

Santiago already weighs four and a half pounds and is growing fast. I'm sure he's much more handsome than this picture shows.

We enjoy getting letters from you, but if it is okay with you and your mother, we'd love to arrange a video call sometime. Your cousins are eager to meet you. Emma and Mia want to hear all about Sundance and the miniature horses you take care of. It's all they ever talk about.

We can't wait to see you over Christmas.

Love,

Daddy

A video call required an internet connection, which they didn't have at Grampy's house. She only had a small amount of data on her phone, so she would have to ask Mom if she could make the call from Olivia and Ryan's house, or maybe from Stephanie's.

Sofia entered her father's cell phone number into her contacts. Mom had agreed to allow her to fly to Florida and meet Daddy over Christmas break. She wouldn't object to a phone call, would she? So why did Sofia feel apprehensive about asking?

Grampy peered over Sofia's shoulder. "How's the baby?"

She showed him the sonogram picture and the letter. Maybe she could ask for his permission to call, instead of Mom's.

Grampy pointed to a shadowy area. "Is that his foot?"

"I thought it was his arm." Sofia examined the picture again. "Because that part is his head, isn't it?"

Grampy shrugged. "At least he's healthy. That's what matters."

Sofia nodded and slid the photo and letter back into the envelope.

"Your mother doesn't get out of work until nine-thirty, so it's just you and me for supper tonight. I've got a box of macaroni and cheese. Or we could have grilled cheese sandwiches." Grampy opened the refrigerator. "Leftover chicken casserole?" He sighed. "I wish Jason could make us something."

"Maybe we should call him," Sofia said, only partially joking. His cooking was much better than Grampy's...and Mom's.

"I like the way you think." Grampy stroked his mustache. "You should call him and tell him you're starving and I'm too old and feeble to make dinner."

"Grampy! You want me to lie?"

"I am old. Maybe not so feeble, but old." He laughed.

"You call him." Sofia held out her phone. "Tell him you're old and sneaky and you want him to make us dinner."

Grampy shook his head. "It would be better coming from you."

Sofia rolled her eyes. "You really are sneaky."

Sofia sat cross-legged on her bed, petting Mrs. Smith's cat, Pumpkin, and waiting for a return text from Jason. The phone buzzed with a call instead.

"Howdy, sunshine," Jason said. "What's this about your sneaky great-grandfather?"

"He wants you to come over to our house and make us dinner."

"I'll tell you what. The two of you can come over here. I was planning on making apple pork chops and a salad for me and Jess. I think I've got some extra pork chops in the freezer, and there's still a half peck of apples from when your mom and I went apple picking last week. How does that sound?"

"Great."

"Tell Mr. Richardson he's a sneaky old guy, but I love him anyway."

"You're the best," Sofia said.

"And don't you forget it."

She ended the call and gave Pumpkin one last scratch under his chin before jumping off the bed. She was halfway to the living room when the thought came to her. Jason's house had Wi-Fi. Maybe she could use Jason's internet connection to make the video call to her father.

The first stars had appeared in the inky sky when Sofia and Grampy pulled into Jason's driveway. Sofia climbed out of the Subaru and looked across the road, but it was too dark to see whether Magic and Rosie were still in their pasture. A dim, yellow light shone through the barn windows. Sofia wondered if Jess was feeding the animals, and, if so, whether she'd allow Sofia to help.

Her stomach rumbled as she followed Grampy to the side porch. Though she looked forward to Jason's cooking, it felt weird to show up without Mom.

Grampy raised his fist, about to rap on the door, when Jason swung it open. "Hello, Mr. Richardson. Hey, Sofia." He wiped his hands on his yellow apron and beckoned them inside. "Dinner's not quite ready, but make yourself at home. Jess is feeding the menagerie."

"Could I help her?" Sofia asked.

Jason smiled. "She's got her system, and always gets annoyed when I show up and mess it up. But I'm sure she wouldn't mind if you offered your help." He slid open the top drawer beside his dishwasher. "It's really dark, though. You should bring a flashlight."

She took it from his outstretched hand and flipped the switch, sending a beam of bright light across the kitchen. Grampy turned to follow Sofia through the door, but she held out a hand to stop him. "I'll be okay by myself."

He nodded. "Careful crossing the road."

She tried not to roll her eyes. "I'll be fine, Grampy. There's probably about two cars an hour on this street."

Jason laughed. "But remember, it's rush hour. I counted eight the other night."

Unsure if he was teasing her or not, Sofia smiled and placed her hand on the doorknob, then hesitated as she remembered her plan to video call Daddy. She needed to ask before she lost her nerve. "I was wondering if I could, uh..." The words stuck in her throat.

Jason gazed at her, one hand clutching a wooden spoon.

"We don't have internet at my house and my father..." She cleared her throat. "He wants to do a video call with me so..."

"You want to use the Wi-Fi," Jason finished. "Of course." He stirred his bubbling pan. "No problem."

"Thanks." Sofia dashed through the door before Jason thought to ask her if Mom was aware of her plan. Mom couldn't object. She shouldn't, anyway. Sofia looked both ways before running across the road and jogging down the hill toward the barn.

Chapter 7

Einstein's booming bark and Harriet's furious yips greeted Sofia as she made her way down Jess's driveway. The dogs leaped through the barn door and bounded up the hill. Einstein's tail thumped enthusiastically, but Harriet growled as she jogged closer.

"Hey, girl, it's just me." Sofia hoped Jason was right about Harriet being all bark and no bite.

"Jason?" Jess's voice called out over the racket.

"It's Sofia!"

"Harriet! Cut it out!" Jess hollered from inside the barn. "Sofia, I didn't know you were coming."

The Boston Terrier yipped a final time before slinking back toward the barn. Einstein nuzzled Sofia's hand and followed her the rest of the way down the driveway.

Sofia peered through the barn door, wondering where Jess was. "We kind of invited ourselves over to Jason's for dinner. Do you need any help?"

Jess appeared from around a corner, hay clinging to her orange fleece jacket and strawberry-blonde hair. "I was just feeding the chickens. Magic and Rosie are already in their stalls, but Tootsie and the goats like to stay outside unless it's freezing. You could throw them some hay, if you'd like."

"How many flakes?" Sofia asked, wondering where Jess kept her hay.

"A flake each. Vincent and Billy probably shouldn't get anything, since they're so fat, but they'll steal Weasel's hay if you don't put any out for them." Jess walked away.

Sofia looked around for a stack of hay bales. A rickety wooden ladder led up to a hayloft over the stalls. Maybe she had to climb up there? She gripped a well-worn rung and gave the ladder a shake. It wobbled ominously, but if Jess could safely climb it, surely Sofia could. She was half-way up when Jess turned around.

"Not up there! Jason and I dropped a bunch of bales the other day. Get hay from that empty stall." She gestured toward a stall opposite Rosie and Magic.

Sofia backed down the ladder, her cheeks blazing. Why hadn't she just asked? Jess must think she was stupid.

She paused in front of Rosie's stall. The Sassy Appy lifted her head from her feed bucket and blinked at her before plunging her nose back into the grain. Magic didn't even look up. Shaking her head, Sofia turned and entered the stall where Jess and Jason had stacked the hay. She searched for an open bale and removed four flakes. She tried to cradle the thick stack of hay against her chest, but one flake slipped from her grasp and tumbled onto the floor.

"Looks like you could use some help," Jess said. "I use a wheelbarrow to carry hay out to their paddock. Sorry, I should have told you. I get into a zone when I'm doing the chores. Jason says I space out on him."

Sofia chewed on her lip and stared at the mess she'd made. Any more mistakes, and Jess would probably banish her from the barn.

"Don't worry about it," Jess said. "I'll get the wheelbarrow."

After loading the hay into the bright yellow wheelbarrow, Sofia followed Jess through a doorway which led directly into the donkey and goat paddock.

"Uh oh. Better cover your ears," Jess warned as Tootsie opened her mouth.

The miniature donkey brayed three times while Sofia laid out separate piles of hay for the animals. She might have laughed if she hadn't felt so nervous about making another mistake.

Pregnant-looking Vincent Van Goat head butted Weasel, pushing him away from his pile. The smaller goat trotted away and found the fourth flake Sofia had spread over the ground. Vincent's pushy behavior reminded her of the way Snickers bossed around Kit Kat. Animals could be so mean to each other, and they didn't even feel guilty about it.

Jess shook her head at Vincent. "I've got to feed the cat. Then we'll be done." She took the empty wheelbarrow and headed back into the barn.

Sofia hurried after her, wishing Jess had given her another job. She hated feeling like a little kid who got in the way instead of helping.

"Josephine." Jess made a kissing sound. "Come and get your din dins."

A skinny calico cat leaped down the hayloft ladder and darted between Sofia's legs. She raced across the barn aisle and into the tack and feed room. As much as Pumpkin loved dinnertime, Sofia couldn't imagine Mrs. Smith's fat orange tabby ever being that fast.

Jess rubbed her hands against her stained sweatpants. "I'm going to make a quick stop in my house, first, since Jason has company. I need to wash up, brush the hay out of my hair, and put on some non-stinky clothing."

"It doesn't matter to me," Sofia said.

"It might matter to your mom, though."

"She's not here. Just me and Grampy."

Jess cocked her head. "I assumed, since you were here... Well, I should still make myself presentable. Are you coming with me or going back to Jason's?"

Sofia fingered the phone in her coat pocket. If she wanted to make a video call tonight, she would need to text her father to ask when he was available. She could text Daddy while Jess was changing. "I'll come with you."

"Okay." Jess whistled, and Einstein and Harriet raced to her side.

Sofia had to jog to keep pace with Jess's quick strides as they headed toward the house.

Unlike the spacious wooden barn, which looked like it might have stood there for one hundred years or more, Jess's house was more like Jason's—a single story ranch, the same size as her brother's, only light blue instead of beige. When she followed Jess inside, she realized they looked exactly the same on the inside, too, except...

"Sorry, it's a bit of a mess." Jess kicked off her muck boots and tossed her orange fleece onto a pile of hats and gloves. She pulled her sweatshirt over her head and added it to the heap. "I'll be right back."

Harriet followed Jess down the hall, but Einstein circled Sofia's legs, bumping his nose against her thighs until she reached down to rub his head. "You're so cute, but I need to text my father." When she withdrew her hand, he pressed his head between her legs. Trying to ignore his attention-seeking antics, Sofia took out her phone. Her pulse quickened as she typed the message.

This is Sofia. I got your letter today. Can we do a video call tonight?

She checked the time. Almost seven. She didn't know how long dinner might take, but it was a school night, and Grampy would want Sofia to be home before Mom finished her work shift. She texted *8:00?*, before she lost her nerve.

Einstein, who'd given up on Sofia, plopped himself onto a squishy dog bed in the cluttered living room. Jess returned from her bedroom, wearing a clean pair of jeans and a flowy, moss green-colored blouse. She'd swept her now hay-free hair into a loose ponytail.

"You look pretty," Sofia said.

Jess smiled. "Thanks. Believe it or not, I usually clean up well. Speaking of which," she glanced at Sofia's hands, "Do you want to clean up before dinner? I mean, who am I to talk, but we are about to eat...of course, maybe you were planning to wash your hands at my brother's house."

Sofia's face flushed. She would have washed her hands before dinner. Probably. Maybe. She nodded and headed for the bathroom, which was located exactly where it was in Jason's house. Jess's sink was considerably less clean than Jason's, however, and there were no guest hand towels hanging on the wall—just a washcloth beside the sink and a bath towel on the floor. Sofia wiped her wet hands on her pants.

Her phone vibrated. Her father's number.

Wonderful! Daniella and I will call at 8. See you soon.

Jason and Grampy were already sitting at the table, their plates filled with pork chops, green beans, rice, and extra slices of cooked apples, when Sofia and Jess walked through the door. Jason raised an empty fork. "We almost gave up and started without you."

Jess picked up an empty plate and scooped out a large serving of rice. "You know my rule. Animals get fed before people."

"But the rule doesn't apply to company," Jason said. "Mr. Richardson, it's okay for you to eat. It's their fault they're so late."

Grampy chuckled. "They're back now. I think I can wait another minute or two."

Sofia's stomach rumbled as she pulled out a chair beside Grampy. As hungry as she was, she wasn't sure how much she could eat. Her father would call in less than an hour. She would hear his voice for the first time since he abandoned her almost eight years ago. What did he sound like? Did he have an accent? She couldn't remember.

Grampy slid a bite of pork and apples into his mouth. "Mmm."

"The sauce has honey and mustard in it," Jason said. "You can put it on the rice, too, if you want."

Sofia ladled the cooked apple mixture over her rice and placed the pork chop on top. It would have been perfect if it hadn't had a bone in it. She cut a few bite-sized pieces.

"Have some beans, too." Jason passed the bowl of green beans.

Sofia wasn't sure if she liked beans, but she put three on her plate, just to be polite. She bit into one, expecting it to be mushy and tasteless, but it crunched in her mouth. "These are good."

Jason smiled. "It puts hair on your chest."

Sofia rolled her eyes and took another bite.

They finished dinner and dessert—Jason had some vanilla ice cream in the freezer—by seven-forty. Sofia still had twenty minutes before her video call. She got up from the table and paced around the living room while Grampy and Jess talked about their favorite sights at Acadia National Park.

"What's up, buttercup?" Jason asked. "Are you nervous about talking with your dad?"

Sofia let out a long breath.

"I bet it feels weird, after all those years." Jason sat on the couch. "Wanna talk about it? Or would you rather be left alone with your thoughts?"

Surprising herself, she nodded and sat beside him. She twisted her hands in her lap. "I want to talk with him, but I'm worried, too. I was angry with him for such a long time, and now that he's in my life again, I'm not sure how to feel. I don't even know anything about him. He's kind of more like an imaginary father, I guess, but now I'm about to talk with him and he's going to become real. That probably makes no sense."

"It does, actually." Jason leaned back against the couch cushions. "The father of your imagination is one person, someone you've known for most of your life. And now that's about to change, because you're going to meet your real-life father. You don't know what to expect or how to feel."

Sofia nodded, wondering if Jason would be upset if she asked about his father. "Jess said your father died when you were in high school."

"He did."

"Do you still think about him?"

Jason sighed. "Yes, though not as often as I used to. I like how you described the feeling of having an imaginary father, because that's kind of what Dad became for me. I used to wonder how he would respond to this or that. Would he approve of me and the directions I was taking in life? I've even had imaginary arguments with him when I didn't think he would agree with my decisions and choices. I still do that sometimes."

Sofia wasn't sure of how to respond. Sorry your father died? Sorry you miss him? She settled on "I'm sorry."

Jason touched her hand and gave it a gentle squeeze. "Don't be sorry. Things are what they are."

He released her hand and stood. "Why don't you use the bedroom across the hall from mine? It's okay to close the door for privacy. I'll ask Jess to help me with the dishes. I can turn up some music. And your Grampy..." Jason grinned. "I've noticed he's a bit on the deaf side, so he probably won't overhear your conversation. Good luck."

Sofia removed her phone from her back pocket to check the time. Fifteen minutes to go. She looked up at Jason, who crossed his eyes and stuck out his tongue. She almost laughed. Then, with her stomach fluttering, she made her way to the spare bedroom and closed the door.

Chapter 8

S ofia settled onto a hard wooden chair in front of Jason's neat
desk. She stared through the window to the dark backyard,
absently tapping her phone against her thigh. Since she had access
to Jason's Wi-Fi, she might as well watch a few silly horse videos
while she waited for the call. A clip of a white horse rolling in a
mud puddle helped to take her mind off the knot hardening in the
pit of her stomach.

Daddy sent a text two minutes before eight o'clock asking if she
was ready. Taking a deep breath, she typed yes.

Sofia was about to see her father for the first time since she was
three and a half years old. She couldn't even remember what he
looked like.

And then he was there, on the tiny screen of her phone, his
toothy, slightly crooked smile wrinkling the corners of his dark
brown eyes—eyes so much like her own. She hadn't forgotten,
after all. The memories of him flooded back. His muscular arms.
His deep voice and booming laugh.

The woman, who must be her stepmother, sat close beside him,
a pretty lady with light brown skin and shiny dark brown hair. Was
Daniella's hair naturally like this, or had she straightened it like
Olivia had once tried and failed to do with Sofia's hair? Daddy's
hair, which had been thick and curly in the sixth-grade school pic-

ture Abuela had sent, was thinner now, and buzzed short, revealing a few strands of white mingling with the dark hair near his temples.

"Sofia! Look at you," he said, with only the slightest hint of a Dominican Spanish accent. "You've grown into such a beautiful young woman."

Sofia shifted in the uncomfortable desk chair, suddenly conscious of how she neither looked nor felt beautiful, at least not like Anika or some of the other girls at school. Mom was beautiful. Daniella was beautiful. Sofia was...a girl with unruly hair who never wore makeup and smelled like horses most of the time.

Daddy continued to beam at her. "This is your stepmother, Daniella."

Daniella waved. "It's so nice to meet you, Sofia."

"Nice to meet you, too." Searching for something else to say, she added, "I like your shirt." Though Sofia would never choose to wear a bright pink top with tropical flowers, it looked nice on Daniella.

"That's so sweet of you. It's covering up my enormous belly."

My brother. "How's the baby?"

Daniella patted her stomach. "Healthy and strong."

Daddy grinned. "Just like his big sister. He'll grow up to be like you. Responsible. A hard worker."

Sofia's cheeks flushed with the compliment.

"Is this your room?" Daddy asked.

Sofia shook her head. She hadn't told her father about Jason. Daddy had married Daniella without even telling her or Mom. Why did she feel awkward admitting that Mom had a boyfriend? "Grampy doesn't have internet at his house so I'm at a friend's place." It was sort of true.

"I didn't think it could be your bedroom," Daniella said. "I'd expect your room to be full of horse show ribbons and trophies."

"I only have three ribbons, and no trophies."

"I'm sure you'll win lots more," Daddy said. "And a great big trophy. The championship. What are the events a young horsewoman competes in?"

"I showed the miniature horses in showmanship, trail obstacle, and jumping." Sofia leaned back in the chair, relieved Daddy had brought up a subject she was comfortable talking about. "Snickers and I weren't very good in showmanship, but I won the jumping class with Kit Kat. I lead the minis over the jumps instead of riding them, since they're so small, but I'm learning how to jump on Sundance. My friend is giving me lessons. She thinks Sundance is a talented jumper and can win at the horse shows next summer."

Daddy and Daniella continued to ask questions about riding and taking care of Sundance. Sofia told them about learning to ride with Gramma Lisa, meeting Stephanie and Grace, joining the Mini Whinnies Horse Club, taking Kit Kat to visit Mrs. Smith in the nursing home, and being invited to ride at Acadia National Park, leaving out the detail about Jason being Mom's boyfriend. "Jess says I can bring a friend with me, but I don't know which one. Ryan isn't a good enough rider. I don't know if I should invite Anika or Olivia."

"Who will be the most fun to ride with?" Daniella asked.

Sofia considered the question for several moments before answering. "Olivia."

"Then you should invite her," Daddy said.

"But I don't want Anika to get upset with me."

"If Anika really is your friend, she'll understand," Daniella said. "Maybe she can go with you the next time."

"Maybe." Sofia wasn't sure if there would be a next time. And she wasn't confident Anika would understand. If it were the other way around, and she picked Anika instead, would Olivia understand? No. Did that mean they weren't her real friends?

Regretting telling Daddy and Daniella about her friendship dilemma, she squirmed uncomfortably on Jason's hard chair.

How long had they been talking? If Sofia and Grampy didn't leave soon, Mom would get home before they did.

"It's been wonderful talking with you, but it's getting late," Daniella said, apparently reading Sofia's thoughts. "Would you like to video chat again sometime soon?"

Sofia nodded. "Maybe Abuela could talk, too?"

Daddy smiled. "I'm sure she'd love to meet you. And Aunt Camila and Uncle Tomas and your cousins, Mia and Daniel and—."

"Don't overwhelm Sofia, Gabriel," Daniella interrupted.

"It's okay," Sofia said. "I want to meet them, too. But, maybe not all at once."

"That's wise. Your father's family can get a bit...loud." Daniella rubbed her manicured hand over Daddy's shoulder. "They all like to talk at once."

"We're just a big, happy family," Daddy said, grinning.

Sofia forced a smile, but her insides churned. *A big happy family I'm not a part of.*

"How did it go?" Jason whispered to Sofia when she entered the living room. Grampy was dozing on the couch while a football game played on the large television screen. Jess must have gone home already.

Sofia sighed. "Good, I guess."

Jason just nodded.

She glanced at Grampy before adding, "But weird, too." She tugged on one of her curls. "They said we can talk again soon. With my grandmother, too. Do you think I could maybe..."

"Do you want to call from here, again?" Jason asked.

"If that's okay."

"You're always welcome at my house. You can use my Wi-Fi anytime. And I'm sure Jess wouldn't mind, if you feel more comfortable calling from her place."

"Thanks. I..." Sofia stared at her shoes. "...I don't know how Mom's going to react to me calling my father and Daniella."

"You didn't tell her?"

"I didn't know it was going to happen until tonight. And it's not like she told me I couldn't call him. It's just that she gets so..." Sofia struggled to find the right words to describe Mom's agitation anytime she mentioned her father and his family. "She's still angry at him."

"He hurt you both a lot," Jason said. "I expect she's afraid he might hurt you again."

"Mom has a hard time forgiving people."

Sofia looked up when Jason gently placed his hand on her shoulder. "Forgiveness is rarely easy," he said. "Give her time."

How much time would Mom need? While thankful for Jason's support and the warmth of his hand on her shoulder, it didn't erase the knot of apprehension coiled in her stomach. "I just hope Mom won't be too upset when she finds out."

Chapter 9

S ofia kicked at a shriveled apple, sending it skidding over the edge of the sidewalk and into the school parking lot. In less than an hour, she'd introduce her friends to Magic and Rosie. Shouldn't she be excited? If Jess approved, they'd have two more horses to ride. She might even allow them to bring Sundance in the horse trailer sometimes, so Anika, Olivia, and Sofia could ride together.

What about Ryan, though? He sat on the bench next to her, slumped over his phone, appearing about as enthusiastic as she felt. He didn't even look up when Olivia joined them.

"I call shotgun," Olivia announced before Pastor Amy's white van pulled up to the curb.

Ryan groaned. "You always do. It's my turn."

"Fine. Take it." Olivia shrugged. "Sofia and I can talk horses in the back seat."

Ryan grabbed his backpack and hurried into the van. He probably worried Olivia might change her mind or whack him with one of her crutches.

Olivia slid open the side door. "I'm bringing my riding helmet in case Jess decides we can ride today."

"I left mine in Stephanie's barn." Sofia lifted her backpack to her shoulder. It was heavy enough without having to haul around her riding equipment. Jess never promised to let them ride today. The arrangement was for Olivia, Ryan, and Anika to meet Jess and introduce them to Rosie and Magic. Sofia hoped her friends wouldn't be as demanding with Jess as they'd frequently been with her.

"You can share my helmet," Olivia offered. "I'll be nice and let Ryan wear it, too, as long as he promises not to give us cooties."

Sofia climbed into the back next to Olivia and buckled her seat belt. "Hi, Pastor Amy. Thanks for picking us up from school."

Pastor Amy turned to look at her. "Thanks for inviting Ryan and Olivia to meet the horses. It's all Olivia has talked about for days."

This didn't surprise Sofia, since it was the only thing Olivia had talked about with *her* since she gave her the news that Jess had agreed to their visit. It was also the only thing Anika had talked about. Ryan was the only one who hadn't constantly brought up the subject.

After they arrived at the Murphy's house, Pastor Amy offered them peanut butter and crackers and glasses of milk. Ryan took his, and sulked off to his room, slamming the door behind him.

"What's up with him?" Sofia asked.

Olivia shrugged. "He's been grumpy since the beginning of the school year. Mom thinks it's teenager hormones."

Pastor Amy sighed. "Instead of talking about him behind his back, maybe you two can check on him."

Sofia's lips tightened. She wasn't talking about Ryan behind his back. She was just asking what was wrong.

Olivia sipped her milk. "If I go in there, he's going to yell at me and tell me to leave him alone."

"I'll talk to him." Sofia left her plate of crackers on the kitchen counter and walked down the carpeted hallway. She hesitated before knocking.

"What do you want?"

"It's Sofia. I just wanted..." What did she want?

"I guess you can come in."

Sofia eased open the door and closed it behind her. Ryan's room was as messy as ever, with a pile of clothes spilling over the end of his unmade bed. He sat at his desk in front of his laptop, staring at the screen. "I'm waiting for the stupid game to load. My computer's a piece of junk."

Sofia considered pointing out that at least he *had* a computer and an internet connection, but that wouldn't help Ryan get out of his foul mood. "What are you playing?"

"Elf Quest." He glanced at Sofia's puzzled face. "It's an old game. I'm probably the only kid at Maplewood who's ever played it, except for..." he swallowed. "Except for Ben McCarthy. His father's the one who told us about it."

Ben was in most of Sofia and Ryan's classes. He always seemed to sneak around, listening in on her conversations. It gave her the creeps. "Olivia told me you used to be best friends." When she saw the pained look on Ryan's face, she immediately regretted her statement.

"We're not anymore."

Sofia desperately wanted to ask what broke up their friendship, but thought better of it. The laptop screen brightened as a flying red dragon flashed into view. "So, what is Elf Quest? What do you have to do to win?"

"Want me to show you?" Ryan broke into a smile, the first Sofia had witnessed today.

"Sure." She looked around the room for a place to sit, finally settling onto the unmade bed.

Ryan explained his elf character's powers and how sapphires gave him energy, but dragons guarded the jewels. "You have to outsmart them before you can steal the gems," he said. "Otherwise, the dragon will blast you with fire and incinerate you."

Sofia pretended to be interested. Maybe if there were horses in the game...

"I have to get over the mountain troll's bridge to get to the—"

Thwack. Thwack. Olivia's crutch beat against the door. "Ryan! Get your butt out here. It's time to go."

Sofia leaped to her feet, glad she didn't have to endure any more commentary about the game.

"I'm showing Sofia something. Just a few more—."

"You're going to make us late!" Olivia burst into the room, her freckled face blazing. "You're showing her that stupid game you and Ben have been obsessed with since fourth grade? Sofia doesn't care about that."

"She asked…" Ryan glanced at Sofia, biting his lip.

Olivia shook her head. "She's just trying to be polite. Sofia doesn't even play video games."

Ryan slumped in his chair. "I thought…"

"It's kind of interesting," Sofia lied. "I mean, I'm glad you showed me." That part was true. She didn't care about old computer games, but it had been nice to see Ryan's mood lighten up. "But we'd better get going."

Ryan frowned. "I think I'll stay here. You can go without me."

"You can't bail on us now." Olivia narrowed her eyes. "Don't tell me you're chickening out."

"I'm not!" Ryan's face reddened.

"No one's going to make you ride," Sofia said. "I don't think Jess is even going to let us."

Ryan sighed. "Okay. I have to change my clothes first."

"You'd better hurry," Olivia huffed. "At this rate, Anika's going to get there before we do."

"I wouldn't worry about that," Sofia said. "She's always late."

"And we're going to be even later if Ryan doesn't get a move on it." Olivia turned and walked through the door.

Sofia forced a smile at Ryan before following her from the room.

"That's Jason's place." Sofia's arm nearly smacked into Ryan's face as she leaned over him and pointed. "Oops. And Jess lives across the road from him. We're almost there."

Olivia pressed her face against the window. "I see the pasture. There's the Appaloosa you told me about. Rosie. And the black horse must be Magic."

Pastor Amy turned down the long driveway leading to Jess's barn.

"Look! Anika's Mercedes." Ryan released the button on his seat belt. "I can't believe she's already here."

Anika stood beside the fence with her arm outstretched, calling to the horses. They must have been running later than Sofia thought. But where was Jess?

Ryan grabbed the door handle. Was he planning to leap from the car while Pastor Amy was still driving down the hill? Had he changed his mind about wanting to ride? Thankfully, he waited until the car stopped—just barely—before jumping out and jogging toward Anika.

Sofia hurried out to join them beside the fence. "How long have you been here?"

Anika shrugged. "A few minutes, maybe? Mum's getting antsy." She leaned closer to Ryan and Sofia, lowering her voice. "I told her this was a Mini Whinnies field trip. I didn't think she'd drive me to a stranger's farm otherwise. Isn't your mom's boyfriend's sister supposed to be here?"

"Jess. Maybe she's not back from work yet."

As if on cue, Jess's enormous black truck appeared at the top of the driveway. Jess waved as she turned toward her house.

"Hey! Why isn't she coming this way?" Olivia shouted as she climbed out from Pastor Amy's van. "Isn't she going to show us the horses?"

"She just got home from work. Give her a minute." Sofia rubbed her temples and let out a sigh.

Anika's mother stepped from her fancy car and slammed the driver's side door closed. "What is going on, Anika? Where are the leaders of your club?"

"Jess is—"

Sofia's words were drowned out by Harriet and Einstein's frantic barking. The dogs barreled toward them.

Ryan stiffened and took several steps backward. Anika's mother shrieked and hurried back into the safety of her car.

"They're friendly, I promise," Sofia called out.

"Einstein! Harriet!" Jess shouted at her dogs as she ran after them.

Einstein reached them first. He circled Sofia's legs, his booming barks demanding attention, until she finally rubbed the top of his yellow head. Harriet joined them a few seconds later.

Anika bent and offered her hand for the Boston Terrier to sniff. "She's so cute."

Ryan let out a noisy breath and stepped toward Harriet with his hand outstretched. When the dog woofed, he squeaked and jerked his hand away.

"Don't be such a scaredy puss." Olivia's crutches clacked on the pavement as she made her way over to the dogs. "She's not going to hurt you."

Ryan glanced at Anika, then looked away, his face reddening.

"Sorry about that." Jess jogged over to them, panting. "They're just excited to have visitors."

Anika's mother made an annoying little *ahem* noise.

"Oh." Jess turned her attention from the dogs. "Where are my manners? You've probably guessed I'm Jason's little sister, Jess."

Anika's mother glanced at Jess's outstretched hand, but didn't take it. "I've never met a person named Jason. I was under the understanding this gathering was a field trip for the Mini Whinnies. Anika joined the club a few weeks ago. Where is Stephanie?"

Sofia glared at her friend, who flashed her a grin. Why had Anika lied to her mother when it was so obvious Mrs. Green would discover the truth as soon as she dropped her off? Then again, Sofia hadn't told Mom about her video call with Daddy and Daniella. She hadn't lied, though. It just never seemed the right time to bring it up.

Jess raised an eyebrow as she glanced at Sofia. "Sofia's told me all about her wonderful little horse club, but..."

Sofia held her breath. *Jess thinks I'm a liar! How can she trust me now?* Would Jess tell Jason? Would he tell Mom? If Mom thought she'd been lying, she might as well kiss the trip to Acadia National Park goodbye.

Chapter 10

Jess's gaze returned to Anika's mother. "Unfortunately, Stephanie couldn't make it this afternoon." She gestured toward the pasture. "I have two horses and a miniature donkey named Tootsie. Since the Mini Whinnies focuses on miniature horses, I'll teach the kids about taking care of Tootsie."

Jess nodded at Sofia, while Mrs. Green scanned the pasture. Did that mean Jess wasn't upset with her, after all?

Mrs. Green turned back. "I don't see a donkey."

"Tootsie's in the pen out back, with the goats. She's too little to be with Magic and Rosie. It wouldn't be safe for her. Or them." Jess flashed a grin at Sofia.

She winced. Anika's lie wasn't funny.

"Since this is a Mini Whinnies field trip, can any of the kids tell me what a female donkey is called?" Jess asked.

Ryan scrunched up his face. "Is it a bad word?"

Anika giggled. "It's called a jenny."

"Three points to…" Jess tilted her head. "I'm sorry. You know my name, but I don't know yours."

"Anika Varna."

"Is that an Indian name?"

"My father was born in India. He moved back there to take care of my grandmother." Anika tossed her sleek, black hair, glaring at her mother. "Mum likes to be called *Mrs. Green*. She's remarried, obviously."

Mrs. Green's lipstick-coated mouth tightened, and her eyes narrowed.

"Nice to meet you, Mrs. Green." Jess turned to Ryan. "And your name is?"

"Ryan Murphy."

"Ryan and Olivia are twins," Anika said. "Their mother is the pastor of the Good Shepherd Community Church."

Pastor Amy was still sitting in her van with the window rolled up. Her phone was pressed against her ear.

"Jess is here, now." Anika flicked her hand at her mother. "You can go home."

"You're welcome to stay and meet the animals," Jess said.

Mrs. Green wrinkled her nose and took a step back. "Thank you for the offer, but I've got some things to do. When should I pick Anika up?"

Jess shrugged. "Maybe an hour?"

"I'm sure we can drive her home," Ryan said. He jogged over to the van and banged on the window. "Mom!"

Startled, Pastor Amy nearly dropped her phone. She rolled down the window, glaring at Ryan. "What?"

"Can we drive Anika home in an hour?"

Mrs. Green glanced at her watch. "I'd appreciate it."

Pastor Amy sighed, then nodded.

Sofia closed her eyes and let out a long breath, annoyed with Anika and Ryan's bossiness and Mrs. Green's rudeness. At least Jess's attention had shifted away from the question of whether this was an official Mini Whinnies field trip.

Jess waited until Pastor Amy's white minivan and Mrs. Green's silver Mercedes turned left at the top of her driveway before placing her hands on her hips. She fixed her gaze on Sofia. "A Mini Whinnies meeting?" She wasn't smiling this time.

Sofia's face flushed. "It wasn't... I didn't..." She glanced at Anika, expecting her to confess to being the source of the lie.

Anika smiled back, saying nothing.

Sofia's gaze darted to Ryan.

He looked away.

"Let's go meet Tootsie," Olivia said. Without waiting for an answer, she headed toward Jess's barn.

Stung by Anika's casual indifference and Ryan's complicit silence, Sofia hurried after her.

When they reached the paddock behind the barn, Anika grabbed Ryan's arm and squealed. "Tootsie is adorable! Look at those ears and her—"

The miniature donkey's bray drowned out whatever else Anika had planned to say. Eyes wide, Ryan leaped backward, pulling Anika with him. She released her grip a moment too late. Arms flailing, she crashed into his shoulder, sending them both tumbling to the ground.

Sofia snorted. Served them right.

Olivia laughed. "That's one loud donkey."

"Watch out," Jess warned, "she's about to—"

Tootsie's second bray was even louder than the first. Sofia covered her ears, grinning.

After visiting with Tootsie and the goats, Jess led Sofia and the others into the barn. "I thought we could bring Rosie and Magic inside to groom them. I'm sure they'll appreciate the attention."

"Can we ride afterward?" Olivia asked. "I brought my helmet. I left it beside the driveway."

"Oh," Anika cried. "Can I borrow it?"

"Your mom said you're not allowed to ride without an instructor," Sofia muttered, not bothering to hide her annoyance.

Anika pouted. "Jess is our instructor. I'm sure—"

"We're just going to groom them today," Jess said. "I want to see how you handle the horses from the ground first."

Ryan blew out a shaky breath. When Anika glanced at him, his cheeks turned pink. Had she realized he was afraid to ride?

Jess grabbed an enormous leather halter from its hook beside Magic's stall and handed it to Sofia. "You and Ryan can get Magic and bring him into the barn. Anika and Olivia can help me get Rosie."

Ryan clasped his hands over his stomach. "The huge, black horse?"

Jess nodded. "That's the one."

He sucked in his lower lip.

"I'll do it and you can just watch," Sofia whispered as they made their way to the horses' pasture. "Unless you want a turn."

"You can do it," Ryan whispered back.

Sofia worried she wouldn't be able to reach Magic's head, even standing on tiptoes, but when she stood by his side the Percheron-cross lowered his head and nuzzled her hand. "Good boy." She slipped the halter around his muzzle and pulled the crown piece behind his ears.

"I can do it myself, Anika." Olivia sounded annoyed.

Sofia glanced in their direction.

Olivia struggled to buckle Rosie's halter as the mare danced sideways. Anika stood only a few inches behind her, her right arm extended over Olivia's head, grasping for the halter.

"I don't want you to get hurt," Anika protested.

"Then get out of my way," Olivia snapped.

Sofia held her breath, hoping Anika would back down before Olivia's simmering anger boiled over.

"I just want to help you," Anika said.

Wrong thing to say.

"I don't need your help!" Olivia screeched.

Rosie's head shot up in alarm. Olivia held onto the halter with one hand and her crutches in the other as the Appaloosa yanked her sideways.

Anika jumped back. "Oh my—"

"Let go!" Jess shouted.

Sofia tightened her grip on Magic's lead rope as the gelding pricked his ears forward, watching the spectacle with curiosity rather than fear. He really was unflappable. But Rosie...

The mare refused to stop moving.

And Olivia refused to let go. "Stand," she commanded, her voice firm. "Woah. Stand."

To Sofia's amazement, Rosie snorted and stopped moving.

Still firmly grasping the halter, Olivia shifted her right leg into a more stable position to support her weight. "That's a good girl," she crooned as she regained her balance.

"Are you alright?" Anika hurried over to Rosie, reaching for the loose end of the lead rope that dangled by Olivia's side.

Olivia snatched the lead with her left hand and scrunched her face. "I already told you, I don't need your help."

"Girls." Jess shook her head.

"What?" Olivia snapped. "I was handling Rosie just fine before Anika—"

"I was only trying to help!" Anika protested.

"Girls," Jess repeated, her tone sharper. "If you don't cut it out, I won't let either of you ride with Sofia at Acadia."

Sofia gasped. *No, no, no!*

But it was too late. Olivia glared at her. "Acadia National Park? Why didn't you tell me?"

"I, uh..." Sofia stammered. "I was going to after...after..."

Anika's eyes widened a moment before a grin spread across her face. "We're going to ride the horses there? Can I ride Rosie?"

"What if *I* want to ride Rosie?" Olivia rubbed her hand down the mare's strawberry roan neck. "Anika can ride Magic. Or Ryan can."

Ryan shook his head. "No, I'm good."

Jess glanced at Sofia and mouthed, *I'm sorry*, before clearing her throat. "I'll be riding Rosie at Acadia."

"But how will we all..." Olivia frowned. "Sofia's riding Sundance, Jess is riding Rosie. That just leaves Magic."

"We're taking turns, then?" Anika asked.

"Either that or Sofia's going to choose between us." Olivia tapped a crutch against the grass.

Sofia wished she could bury her blazing face in Magic's mane. Jess and Jason had told her she could bring *one* friend. Would they allow both Anika and Olivia to come on the trip? If they did, she'd have to invite Ryan, too, even if he didn't want to ride.

How would Mom and Grampy react if Anika, Olivia, and Ryan joined their *family* trip? She swallowed, imagining her friends' constant bickering. Mom and Grampy would hate it.

So would Sofia.

Inviting all of them would be a nightmare. She'd have to choose between Olivia and Anika. And when she did, one of them would never forgive her.

Chapter 11

Ryan once claimed Anika's family was so wealthy they had a swimming pool *inside* their house. He must have been mistaken, because as they turned down Anika's tree-lined driveway, Sofia spotted a fenced-in swimming pool and gazebo to the right of the massive, three-story Colonial-style home. Surely, even a rich family wouldn't own *two* swimming pools.

Pastor Amy parked the van in front of a three-bay garage. Anika unfastened her seatbelt. "Thanks for the ride," she said as she stepped out of the van.

Ryan lurched forward from the back seat. "Can we see your house?"

Anika looked over her shoulder and shrugged. "I guess."

Pastor Amy sighed. "Ryan, it's getting late. I need to make dinner before leading the Bible study tonight."

"It won't take long, Mom." Ryan hopped out of the van.

"Sofia, aren't you coming, too?" Anika called out.

Sofia glanced at the back of Pastor Amy's head, unsure whether she would scold them for keeping her waiting in the van. Olivia remained motionless beside her mother. "Are you coming, Olivia?" Sofia asked.

"I wasn't invited," she snapped.

"Don't be stupid," Ryan said. "Come and see her house with us."

"Not if I'm not invited." Olivia folded her arms over her chest.

Anika rolled her eyes. "Olivia, do you want to come inside with us?"

"I guess, seeing as everyone else is going."

"Please come right back," Pastor Amy pleaded.

Sofia clenched her fists inside her coat pockets and counted to three before letting out a long breath. Olivia and Ryan's bickering annoyed her, but they rarely stayed angry with each other for long. The tension between Anika and Olivia, however, showed no signs of cooling. The revelation that she must choose between her two friends had only escalated their rivalry.

Ryan hurried after Anika while Sofia waited for Olivia to get out of the van. "Thanks for waiting for me, Anika," Olivia muttered under her breath.

Sofia sighed again, hoping Olivia would get the hint. She was in no mood to listen to Olivia's complaints, even if they were justified.

"Since you're getting the grand tour, Mum would want me to take you through the front instead of the garage." Leading the way, Anika directed them to a covered porch that stretched from one end of the house to the other. Two sturdy columns flanked the entrance. At the top of the steps, she turned back to stare at Olivia. "Can you make it up the stairs?"

"I climb stairs all the time," Olivia barked.

"Sorry, I..." Anika looked away. "...was just trying to be considerate."

Ryan glared at his sister. "You don't have to be such a jerk."

"Why don't you mind your own business?" Olivia said.

Ryan had a point, but Sofia didn't dare to agree with him out loud. She took a deep breath before following a step behind Olivia. At least she couldn't be accused of *not waiting* for her friend.

Anika punched a code into a panel mounted on the front door. It made a faint whirring noise, followed by a click. She turned the handle, opening the door to reveal a spacious entryway with hardwood floors and stairs leading up to the second floor.

"We don't usually come in this way, so there isn't a place to leave our shoes." Ankia bent to remove her boots. "Mum and Andrew would freak out if we didn't take off our barn shoes, though."

Ryan kicked off his sneakers, leaving a clump of dried mud on the previously spotless floor. Sofia placed her paddock boots more carefully, self-conscious of the caked-on dirt and horse manure clinging to the treads.

Olivia stared at Ryan's mess and blew out a frustrated breath. Was she going to yell at him? Sofia bit her lip.

"It's hard for me to take off my boots when I'm standing." Olivia's voice was barely above a whisper.

"Oh! I'll get a chair from the dining room." Anika darted through an opening to the right. She returned a moment later with a high-backed, upholstered chair that looked like a miniature version of a king's throne. She placed the chair beside Olivia without making eye contact.

Sofia looked away, too, unsure of whether she was more embarrassed for Olivia's sake or Anika's.

Ryan broke the awkward silence. "I want to see your swimming pool."

Anika glanced at Olivia from the corner of her eye. "Uh, we just took off our shoes."

"I mean the inside one," Ryan said.

"Do you mean our jacuzzi? The hot tub?" Anika laughed.

Ryan's face flushed pink. "Yeah. That."

After their tour of Anika's humongous house, including the indoor *jacuzzi*, which looked more like an enormous bathtub than a swimming pool but smelled faintly of chlorine, Anika tapped Sofia on the shoulder. "Can I talk with you in private for a second?"

"Pastor Amy's waiting for us." Sofia hoped this excuse would deter Anika from asking the question she'd probably been eager to ask since Jess had mentioned the Acadia trip.

"It will only take a second," Anika insisted. Without waiting for a response, she launched into her pitch. "I know you and Olivia are best friends, and it's not nice to judge someone with a disability, but..."

Then maybe you shouldn't judge her. Sofia's cheeks grew hot. *Say it! Just say it!* Why couldn't she stand up for her friend? She'd done it before, but her courage was failing her now, perhaps because she knew Olivia would make a similar request the moment they were alone together.

"Don't you think it's going to be difficult for Olivia to ride Magic at Acadia?" Anika asked. "I'm not saying she doesn't know how to ride, but riding a therapy horse inside an indoor ring is totally different from being out on a trail."

Sofia swallowed. As much as it annoyed her to hear Anika express this opinion, she'd worried about the same thing. Magic was a calm horse, but anything could happen on the trail. He could spook at a bicycle or lose his footing and stumble. He might react badly to the feeling of Olivia's leg braces pressing against his sides. And if she fell off...

"You'll want to trot and canter on your ride. She might hold you back." Anika glanced out the door. Ryan and Olivia had already climbed into the van. "Just think about it."

Sofia nodded and hurried to the van, dreading Olivia's inevitable question.

"What did Anika want to talk with you about?"

"Nothing. Just...something about our...Spanish assignment." *You're a liar, Sofia Ruiz.*

"She should ask me for help," Ryan said.

Olivia snorted. "You? You've got to be kidding. I probably know more Spanish than you do, and I'm taking French."

Now Sofia would have to send Anika a text as soon as she got home. Lying to Olivia was bad enough. Being caught in a lie? She didn't want to think about it.

"So," Olivia said, "about that Acadia trip..."

The setting sun bathed Sundance's palomino coat in warm golden highlights. Stephanie had already mucked out the stalls, telling Sofia to spend the few remaining minutes of daylight riding her horse.

"I think you could use some time in the saddle," Stephanie had insisted when Sofia offered to finish the chores. "Hard day? You look stressed out."

Sofia had simply nodded without offering an explanation, and Stephanie hadn't pressed her for more information. Sofia appreciated that about Stephanie. Unlike most grownups, she didn't expect Sofia to share the details of her problems or feelings if she didn't feel like talking about them.

Stephanie now sat at the picnic table, cradling a mug of coffee between her gloved hands.

"Can I take Sundance over a few cross rails after we warm up?" Sofia asked.

"You'd both enjoy that," Stephanie said, "but you'd better get going. If you wait too much longer, you won't to be able to see the jumps!"

Sofia nodded and urged her horse into a trot. As they circled the paddock, she tried to push thoughts of the Acadia trip from her mind. She needed to focus her attention on riding Sundance well and practicing her form over small jumps. The choice between Anika and Olivia could wait.

She rode a figure-eight at the trot, balancing in two-point position with her weight fully resting in the stirrups instead of the saddle. With her back held straight and heels pressed down, she resisted the temptation to slouch, even as her upper body tilted forward.

"Your jumping position looks great," Stephanie called out from the picnic table. "Your balance has really improved."

Thanks to Anika's help. If it hadn't been for Anika, she wouldn't have learned how to ride in two-point position—or discovered Sundance's talent for jumping. As frustrating as Anika could be sometimes, she had enthusiastically guided Sofia over the past few weeks, and not just with riding. Anika had welcomed her to Maplewood Middle School and taken her under her wing. She'd introduced Sofia to her many popular friends. Some still acted snobby or aloof around Sofia, but others were beginning to treat her like a friend, too.

And, as rich as Anika was, she didn't own a horse. Her mother had forced her to quit riding after a bad fall. While she had recently agreed to her daughter riding under the supervision of an instructor, she remained firm in denying Anika's request for riding lessons. No wonder she'd been so desperate to ride Rosie or Magic.

Olivia rode Molly every week during her therapeutic lesson, and she frequently rode Sundance, too. Now she assumed Sofia would invite her to ride Magic during the Acadia trip.

"Aren't you going to take a few cross rails?" Stephanie asked.

Sofia blinked. How long had she been circling the paddock? With a sigh, she trotted toward the jump.

Chapter 12

"Doesn't she look stunning?" Mom reached for Sofia's hand, beaming. "This soft pink is such a nice color on her. I wish she'd dress up more often."

Jason stroked his scraggly red beard, grinning. "It's a beautiful dress, though I expect she'd rather be wearing jeans and sneakers."

"Don't be silly. All the girls will be dressed like this." Mom squeezed Sofia's hand. "And Sofia will be the prettiest one."

Sofia wished Mom would stop talking about her like she wasn't standing right there. She tugged on the frilly hem that only reached half-way down her thighs. When she'd told Mom about Anika's birthday party, Mom had insisted on taking her shopping.

Grampy frowned, shaking his head. "The dress is awfully short."

Sofia silently agreed, but Mom was right, at least according to Olivia. All the girls at Anika's party would wear dresses like this, and many would be even shorter than Sofia's.

At the sound of the doorbell, she yanked her fingers free from Mom's grasp and hurried to the door.

"You look great," Olivia said as she stepped inside. She wore a silky, dark-green dress. She'd straightened her curly red hair, which now cascaded in soft waves over her bare shoulders.

"So do you." Sofia willed herself not to stare at her friend's leg braces. She'd seen them many times, of course, but never paired with an elegant dress.

Ryan trudged up the steps behind his sister, wearing the suit and tie he'd worn for the showmanship class at the miniature horse show in August. Sofia doubted the other boys would dress so nicely. "We need to hurry," he said. "The party started ten minutes ago."

"Not before pictures," Mom chided. "I want a few with just Olivia and Sofia. Then all three of you."

Ryan sighed. "We're already late."

"Sorry, man." Jason chuckled. "You're going to be stuck here for a while."

"But the party started—"

"I already told you." Olivia rolled her eyes. "Only dorks show up to parties like this early."

But when they arrived at Anika's house half an hour later, the enormous front entryway was already packed so full of classmates that they could barely pass through the door. Sofia hesitated just inside the entrance, wondering if she'd be better off turning around and chasing Pastor Amy's van down the driveway. If she did, she'd probably trip in Mom's heels and end up falling flat on her face, but it might be less awkward than navigating through the swarm of sixth and seventh graders.

Olivia gave Sofia's shoulder a nudge. "Come on."

Chloe, the friendliest of Anika's gang, waved to Sofia from the other side of the hallway. "I love your dress," she called out over the loud music.

Hope and Lily, two of Anika's less than welcoming friends, gestured toward Olivia's legs, not bothering to hide their giggles. Sofia shot them an angry glare as Olivia straightened her back and lifted her chin.

"Where's Anika?" Ryan pushed past Sofia and Olivia and shoved his way through the crowd.

"Nice suit!" Hope shouted as Lily snorted by her side. Most of the guests were girls, but the few boys Sofia spotted were dressed in more casual clothing. A few wore button-down dress shirts, but none were wearing jackets and ties like Ryan.

Taking Olivia's lead, Sofia ignored Hope and Lily's rude behavior and made her way toward Chloe and a girl named Mia, who Sofia knew from Spanish class. "That's a great color on you," Chloe said to Olivia.

"I know." Olivia grinned.

"There's apple cider donuts in the kitchen," Mia said. "Assuming *James* hasn't eaten them all."

"James is here?" Sofia couldn't believe Anika would invite the bully to her party after everything that had happened a few weeks earlier. After picking on Ryan for months, James had shoved him against a locker at school and warned him to stay away from Anika. When Anika told James to leave him alone because Ryan was her friend, James had been furious.

Chloe nodded. "He came with *Emily*."

"My two favorite people," Olivia said, her voice dripping with sarcasm.

"Yeah, mine, too." Mia brushed her sleek brown hair over her bare shoulder. "It's bad enough to deal with them at school."

Sofia should warn Ryan, who was making his way into the kitchen. "Where is he?"

Chloe shrugged. "Probably still scarfing down all the food in the kitchen."

"Happy birthday, Anika!" Ryan shouted over the music. "I brought you a present!"

Oh no! Sofia hurried after Ryan to tell him to watch out for James, but it was already too late.

"What are *you* doing here?" James snarled. He lunged toward Ryan, his blond hair brushing against his broad shoulders.

Ryan recoiled, colliding with his ex-best friend, Ben, who shoved him to the side. What was *Ben* doing here? Had Anika invited everyone from Maplewood Middle School?

Sofia balled her fists. She'd stood up to James twice before. She could do it again—as long as she didn't allow herself time to think about it. "He's here because Anika invited him. They're friends."

James narrowed his eyes and wrinkled his nose, but didn't contradict Sofia's claim. Instead, he attempted to snatch Anika's present from Ryan's hands. "What did you get her?"

Ryan clutched the package against his chest. "None of your business."

Ben pushed his glasses up the bridge of his nose and grinned. "Ryan has a crush on Anika."

Ryan's cheeks flushed bright pink. "I do not."

Startled, Sofia wondered if Ben might be right. Could Ryan have a crush on Anika, the prettiest, most popular girl in the sixth grade? The girl James had a crush on, too, even though he was dating Emily?

Ben's grin widened. "You can't deny it. I see the way you look at her at school. That's why you brought her a present. And why you're all dressed up."

"Shut up, Ben." Sofia turned to the sound of Olivia's voice. "My brother brought a present for Anika because it's her *birthday*. That's what friends do."

Chloe nodded. "I brought her a present. So did Mia."

Sofia bit her lip. Why hadn't she brought Anika a gift? Maybe she'd have to promise to give her a ride on Sundance...or take her to Acadia with her.

Anika glided into the kitchen, accompanied by giggling Hope and snickering Lily. Her strapless purple dress sparkled with sequins, and her sleek black hair had been swept up in an elegant updo. "Ryan! You're all dressed up!" She glanced at James, fingering a loose lock of hair that brushed her cheek.

Ryan's face blazed an even brighter shade of pink. James' cheeks nearly matched.

"You brought me a present?" Anika held out her hands. Her fingernails were painted purple to match her dress.

Ryan glanced at Ben, who smirked back at him, before handing the gift to Anika. "I... I hope you like it."

Sofia held her breath while Anika slid her finger under the wrapping paper. She gently pulled it off, revealing a framed picture.

Anika gazed at it for a moment, her grin widening. "Did you paint this?"

Ryan nodded. "It's watercolor."

Anika studied the painting. "Is this me standing next to Kit Kat?"

"At the nursing home," Ryan said. "When we visited Mrs. Smith."

"Kit Kat's wearing her adorable blue sneakers." Anika looked up at Ryan. "This is amazing. I can't believe you painted this for me. You're so talented."

Ryan ducked his head. "Thanks."

"Let me see it." Lily grabbed the frame from Anika's hands. "Kit Kat is so small. Is she a miniature horse or something?"

"Yeah," Anika said. "Ryan and Olivia and Sofia and I are in this miniature horse club together. We're the Mini Whinnies."

James snorted. "The Mini *Weenies.*"

Ben snickered.

Olivia narrowed her eyes at him before glaring at James. "Maybe you and Ben are the mini weenies, but we're the Mini Whinnies."

Anika covered her mouth, unable to contain her giggles.

"Good one," Ryan whispered to his sister.

"I know," Olivia said, grinning. She elbowed Sofia in the ribs. "Come on. You've got to admit that was funny."

Sofia nodded, her gaze darting from red-faced Ben to scowling James before resting on pink-cheeked Ryan. Only a month ago, he'd openly disliked and distrusted Anika. They'd become friends through the Mini Whinnies, but something more had grown between them, or at least something was different in the way Ryan acted around her. He'd been moody since the end of the summer, frequently brooding in his room, unenthusiastic about joining Olivia and Sofia at the barn, unless.... Unless Anika was going to be there.

"Thank you for the painting," Anika said when their laughter finally died down. She wrapped her left arm around Ryan's shoulders. "It's the best gift ever."

Ryan leaned into her one-armed hug, beaming.

It was true! Ryan had a crush on Anika!

Did she like him back? Sofia wasn't sure. Anika was friendly with almost everyone, including James. She'd even suspected Anika might have a bit of a crush on James, despite the fact he was a nasty bully. Was that why she'd invited him to her party? Or had he come as Emily's date, as Chloe suggested?

Sofia sighed, frustrated by the drama swirling around her and wishing she could be at the barn with Sundance.

"How was the party?" Pastor Amy asked when Sofia, Olivia, and Ryan climbed into the van.

"Great!" Ryan grinned at Sofia as he buckled his seatbelt. "Anika really liked my painting. She's going to hang it in her bedroom."

"You should have seen her dress, Mom," Olivia said. "It was gorgeous. And she was wearing a lot of makeup, too. Most of the girls were. Why won't you let me? I'm almost twelve."

"You won't be twelve until March. And twelve is still much too young." Pastor Amy looked over her shoulder as she backed up the van. "Did you have a good time, Sofia?"

She almost shrugged, catching herself just in time. "Yes." It wasn't exactly a lie. Anika and Olivia seemed to be getting along again, and neither had brought up the subject of riding Magic at Acadia. Chloe and Mia had been friendly, allowing Sofia, Olivia, and Ryan to hang out with them for most of the evening. James had stormed out with Emily shortly after he'd tried to bully Ryan, and Ben had avoided him for the rest of the night.

So, why were Sofia's insides churning?

Olivia turned from her usual spot in the front passenger seat. "I was thinking about Acadia. It's not fair for you to have to choose between me and Anika."

Sofia's stomach lurched. *That's why.* That and the fact that Ryan was in love with Anika. Sofia took a deep breath, certain Olivia's proposal wouldn't include the words *"It's okay if you don't invite me."*

"We haven't always gotten along that great," Olivia continued, "but Anika is a decent person. I'm sure we can work something out. Like I ride on Friday afternoon, and she can ride on Saturday. And Ryan can ride on Sunday morning if he wants."

Ryan bit his lip. "Do I have to ride? Maybe you can take my place, and I can hang out with Anika."

"That sounds like a good compromise," Pastor Amy said.

"Uh..." Sofia gripped the hem of her frilly dress to keep her hands from shaking. *A good compromise?* Who she invited to Acadia was Sofia's choice, not Olivia's. Not Anika's. Not Ryan's. And certainly not Pastor Amy's.

Not knowing how else to respond, she muttered, "I'll think about it."

Chapter 13

"I don't know what to do." Sofia shivered and rubbed her arms against the early dawn chill. A thin layer of frost coated the grass in Sundance's pasture. "The trip is supposed to be fun. Jason and Jess say we're going to love it. Is it bad that I wish they'd never invited me?"

Sundance blew out a fluttery breath. Steam rose from his nostrils.

"It's not you," Sofia quickly added. She stroked her horse's fuzzy neck. "I want to ride you in Acadia. I just don't want my friends to come, too."

Why not? Since Anika's party last night, they were finally getting along. They could take turns riding Magic. Ryan would keep Olivia company when Anika was riding, and he'd be more than happy to hang out with Anika when Olivia was riding.

Sofia unbuckled Sundance's halter. He nuzzled her coat pocket, searching for the piece of carrot she'd hidden inside.

"You're worse than Snickers," she teased as she reached into her pocket. "Here you go."

Sundance's lips brushed over her palm. His breath warmed her numb fingers as he swept the treat into his mouth. He chewed, swallowed, and looked at her expectantly.

"That's all I've got, silly."

He stood there another moment, blinking his large brown eyes, before turning and trotting away.

Sofia checked her phone. 7:12. She still had a couple of hours to spare before she and Grampy needed to leave for church. It would only take her twenty or thirty minutes to finish the barn chores. What if she rode Sundance after she finished mucking out the stalls? Since Stephanie didn't go to church, she might be willing to supervise her.

She sighed. Riding in circles in the makeshift riding ring wasn't very exciting, even if she added a few jumps. What they really needed—or at least what Sofia wanted—was a trail ride, but they didn't have anyone to ride *with*.

What about Jason? Would he be willing to bring Magic in the trailer so they could ride together like they had two weeks earlier? Might Jess come, too, with Rosie?

Sofia wouldn't be able to attend church if she rode with Jason and Jess this morning. Olivia would expect to see her at worship, and would complain about being left out of the plan. But if Sofia waited until the afternoon, Olivia would expect an invitation. And, if Anika found out, she'd expect an invitation, too.

Maybe Jason could help her find the courage to tell her friends what they didn't want to hear. Would it be weird if she called him?

She stared at her phone screen. She *could* call Daddy and ask him for advice, but he'd never met Olivia, Ryan, and Anika. He didn't know Jason or Jess. He barely knew Grampy or Gramma Lisa or any of Sofia's family.

She swallowed, realizing Daddy could say the same about *her*. She didn't know anyone on her father's side of her family. But whose fault was that? Not Sofia's.

Her phone dimmed, but rather than putting it back into her pocket, she tapped her finger on the screen, sending it back to its full brightness.

What about Gramma Lisa? She would know what to do.

Sofia pressed the icon next to her grandmother's name. After the third ring, she expected the call to go to voicemail, but then Gramma Lisa's low, rumbly voice called out. "Sofia! Is everything alright?" She sounded like she was out of breath.

"I'm fine," Sofia said, feeling slightly guilty as she realized how long it had been since she'd called or texted. She hadn't even told Gramma Lisa about the Acadia trip. "How are you?"

"Doing fine, though I'm missing my barn helper." She laughed. "I'm just finishing up Delilah's stall. That mare can sure make a mess of things. She peed on her hay again. With the price of hay what it is, Little Miss Piggy's going to send me to the poorhouse."

Sofia smiled at the mention of Delilah's nickname. "I miss her. And you."

"So, what's going on with you and Sundance? Are you still taking jumping lessons with Anika? You need to send me more pictures. And updates."

"Sorry. I've been kind of..." Sofia shivered and stomped her feet. Maybe it wasn't the best idea to chat on the phone in Sundance's pasture when it was only 38 degrees outside. At least no one would overhear her conversation.

"Busy?" Gramma Lisa suggested.

"Yeah." Sofia gazed at Sundance, who nibbled on what little remained of the frosty pasture grass instead of eating from the pile of hay she'd set out for him. "You know Mom's new boyfriend, Jason?"

Gramma Lisa sighed. "I knew it. He's turned out to be a jerk, just like they all do."

"No!"

Sundance's head shot up. He stared wide-eyed at Sofia.

"No," Sofia repeated, her voice softer. "Jason is really nice. So is his sister, Jess. They've invited me, Grampy, and Mom to go up to Acadia National Park on Veteran's Day weekend. The park has lots of carriage trails for horseback riding. Jess is bringing her horse, and I can bring Sundance."

"Oh, Sofia, that sounds lovely."

"They can bring their horse, Magic, too. Jason was going to ride him, but Mom got...uh...kind of annoyed about that, so he's going to hang out with her instead."

"Figures," Gramma Lisa muttered.

"Jason said I can invite a friend to ride Magic. Only, I don't know who to choose. Olivia or Anika."

"Who do you like better?"

Sofia shrugged. "Olivia can be bossy sometimes, but she's my best friend. Anika is a better rider, but she can be pushy, too, in a different way. If I choose Anika, Olivia will be mad, and if I choose Olivia, Anika will be disappointed and might not want to be my friend anymore. Olivia thinks I should invite both of them, and Ryan, too. Ryan's too scared to ride, but he's got a crush on Anika, so he wants to come."

"Quite the conundrum." Gramma Lisa chuckled. "Is that what you want to do, then? To invite all three of them?"

"Would I be a horrible friend if I said no?"

Gramma Lisa chuckled again. "Not at all. It sounds like way too much drama, if you ask me. Dealing with your mom is going to be plenty to handle as it is."

Sofia let out a breath. "But if I say no to them, they'll hate me."

"If they're your true friends, they'll respect your decision."

Hadn't Daniella said nearly the same thing?

Maybe it was true. If they were her real friends, they should accept her choice not to include them. It would be a lot easier if she gave them a reason they couldn't come, however, like how it was a family trip, not a friend trip. Unfortunately, they knew Jess would allow Sofia to bring a friend.

Unless...

"Gramma Lisa? Would you like to ride with me at Acadia?"

Sofia hurried down the hill to Stephanie's barn. The conversation with Gramma Lisa had taken a lot longer than she'd expected, and she still had three stalls to muck out.

Gramma Lisa hadn't been sure, at first. Delilah would have to travel over six hours in the horse trailer to get to Acadia, assuming they didn't get stuck in traffic or need to make more than a quick stop or two along the way. "It's a big trip," she'd explained, "and a lot to expect of her. She'd have to cart me around the trails for three days and then travel another six hours home."

"What if you rode Magic, instead?" Sofia had asked. That way, Olivia and Anika wouldn't have a horse to fight over, and Sofia's problem would be solved. She held her breath while Gramma Lisa deliberated.

"As long as I can find someone to take care of Delilah over the weekend," Gramma Lisa had finally decided. "I'll ask Anna. She's always glad to earn a few extra dollars for her college fund."

Sofia grabbed the manure fork from its place against the barn wall and tossed it into the empty wheelbarrow. She'd tackle Sundance's stall first, since it was the messiest. Halfway through, her phone pinged with a message from Olivia.

Are you still coming to church? Mom says we can stay home and sleep in because of Anika's party.

Sleep in? Sofia snorted. You didn't get to sleep in when you had horses to care for.

Not sure, she texted back, relieved Pastor Amy—and Olivia—didn't expect her to attend church today. Sofia could avoid her friends' awkward conversations for a few more hours.

Chapter 14

Grampy frowned when Sofia informed him she wouldn't be coming to church. "Are you sure?" he asked. "I heard Mrs. Smith baked more peanut butter cookies. And she'll be expecting an update about Pumpkin."

Sofia tugged at a curl that had come loose from her ponytail. She'd forgotten about Mrs. Smith. Would she be letting her elderly friend down if she skipped church this week? "I was hoping Jason and Jess would ride with me. We need to get the horses into shape for our trip to Acadia."

"Can't you ride this afternoon? It will be warmer."

Sofia sighed. Grampy was probably right, but she was unwilling to admit it. "I'll ask Jason."

Grampy hesitated. "Maybe you should check with your mother first."

"Check with me about what?" Mom padded into the kitchen, wearing bright pink flannel pajamas and matching slippers. She opened a cabinet beside the sink, took out a mug, and yawned.

"Sofia would like to call Jason," Grampy said.

Mom poured coffee into the mug, grinning. "Should I be jealous?"

"No, Mom. Gross." Sofia wrinkled her nose. "I just wanted to see if he and Jess would ride with me today."

"I'm sure he would," Mom said. "I'm so happy you two have hit it off."

"Me too," Sofia admitted. She'd disliked all of Mom's previous boyfriends, especially Paul, who'd planned to marry Mom and send Sofia to boarding school in England. Jason was about as opposite from Paul as a person could be. Instead of being snobby and controlling, like Paul, or distant and indifferent, like Patrick, Jason genuinely cared about her, treating her with kindness and even...dare she think it? *Love?* Like he saw Sofia as part of his family.

Mom placed her coffee mug on the kitchen counter. "Would you like me to call and ask Jason for you?"

Sofia shook her head. If Mom got on the phone with him, she'd have to listen to her say all kinds of embarrassing, mushy stuff while she waited for an answer about going on a trail ride. "Is it okay I call?"

"Sure, Honey Bear."

"Hey, Sofia. What's up?" Jason asked, sounding concerned.

She shifted on her chair and jiggled her foot, suddenly aware of how strange it was to be calling her mother's boyfriend at 8:30 on a Sunday morning. Had she woken him from sleep? "Nothing's wrong. I was just wondering if Sundance and I could ride with you this morning. Like maybe you can bring Magic over in the trailer. Jess and Rosie could come, too."

"That would be fun," Jason said, "But don't you have church?"

Sofia hadn't expected this question from Jason. Did he attend church somewhere, too? She'd never thought to ask. "I don't have to go this morning. Pastor Amy is allowing Olivia and Ryan to sleep in, since we were up late at Anika's party."

"The pastor's kids don't have to go to church? What's this world coming to?" Jason laughed.

Sofia didn't know how to answer.

"But your Grampy is going, isn't he?"

"Yeah, he always goes, but he doesn't force me to come with him."

"Force?" Jason laughed again. "No, I expect not. But what would Grampy think of me if I agreed to ride with you on a Sunday morning instead of coming to church with you?"

Sofia blinked. "You want to go to church with me and Grampy?"

"And your mother, of course. After church, we can go out for lunch and *then* we can ride. That's the proper way to do it, don't you think?"

"Uh... I guess?"

"Great! I'll pick you up in an hour. Tell your mom I expect her to be ready on time. No excuses."

Sofia stared at her phone for several seconds after he ended the call. What had just happened? She'd called Jason hoping to *avoid* going to church and possibly running into Olivia, who hadn't said whether she planned to sleep in. Now Sofia would be attending with Grampy, Jason,and Mom.

Mom nearly spat out her coffee when Sofia informed her that Jason would arrive in exactly one hour to take them all to church. "He wanted me to tell you he expects you to be ready on time," Sofia said, unable to suppress a grin as Mom stared at her in disbelief.

Grampy's mustache twitched. "The young man has his priorities straight."

Mom shook her head. "He's just trying to impress you."

"It worked," Grampy said, "Though I expect there's more to it than that."

He wants us to be a family. Sofia's stomach fluttered as the thought danced in her mind. Could it be true?

Mom pushed her chair away from the kitchen table and stood. "What should I wear?"

Sofia shrugged. "Whatever you want. You don't have to dress up or anything, though you might want to change out of your pink pajamas."

"I think they're kind of cute." Mom smiled. "But I need a shower. And you do, too."

The doorbell rang at 9:27. Sofia sprang from the living room couch and hurried to the door. "Mom's not ready yet," she told Jason, rolling her eyes. "She's still putting on her makeup."

"She's got three minutes." Jason tapped his wrist. "If she's not ready by then, I'm leaving without her."

"You wouldn't do that," Sofia said.

Jason smirked and wandered into the living room. "Good morning, Mr. Richardson."

"Good morning," Grampy said as he rose from his well-worn, plaid recliner. "Good Shepherd Community Church isn't that formal. You don't need to wear a tie."

Jason tugged at the navy blue, silky material around his neck. "My father would roll over in his grave if I didn't wear a tie to church."

Grampy laughed. "I'd better go put on one, then, or you're going to make me look bad."

"Oh, no, Mr. Richardson." Jason quickly loosened his tie. "I didn't mean to—"

"Stop." Grampy shook his head. "Keep it on. I'm just teasing you, Jason."

An involuntary giggle bubbled from Sofia's lips. "I'll tell Mom to hurry." She dashed from the room and down the hallway. Mom was right. Jason *was* trying to impress Grampy.

And clearly, Mom was trying to impress Jason. She wore a flowy, knee-length black dress and had swept her long, blonde hair into a stylish updo, similar to the way Anika had styled her hair for her party. Mom applied a layer of mascara to her pale eyelashes before looking away from the mirror. "You're lucky you have such naturally long, thick lashes," Mom said. "You won't even need to wear mascara when you're older."

Sofia had no intention of wearing makeup, *ever*, but it didn't seem the right time to mention it. Instead, she said, "You look pretty."

Mom smiled. "Thank you."

"Jason dressed up, too," Sofia added. "He's wearing a tie!"

Mom's grin widened as she opened a tube of bright pink lipstick. "Do you think this is a good shade? Or should I wear something darker?"

Sofia groaned. "He's going to leave without you if you aren't ready to leave in one minute."

"He won't leave without me."

"Yes, I will."

Both Mom and Sofia jumped at the sound of Jason's voice. He stood on the other side of Mom's open bedroom doorway with his arms crossed over his chest. "You look gorgeous as always, Mandi, but God doesn't care what color your lips are."

Sofia snorted.

Mom tutted. "Whose side are you on, Sofia?"

"God's side," Jason replied, grinning.

"Fine," Mom said. "Let me put on some lipstick and grab my heels. I'll be ready in two minutes."

Jason shook his head. "Better make it thirty seconds. Mr. Richardson is already getting into my truck. There's no way I'm making him late for church."

Laughing, Sofia thrust Mom's black pumps into her hands. "You can put your lipstick on in the car."

They were going to church together.

As a family.

Chapter 15

Remembering Jason's promise to take them out for lunch, Sofia limited herself to one of Mrs. Smith's peanut butter and chocolate kiss cookies. Without Ryan and Olivia at church to hoard them in Pastor Amy's office, the cookie platter was considerably fuller than it had been last Sunday.

"Don't ruin your appetite," Mom chided when she noticed the cookie in Sofia's hand.

Sofia groaned and was about to stomp away when Jason brushed his hand over her shoulder. "My motto is 'eat dessert first'. You should never pass up a homemade cookie, especially if it's made with peanut butter. Do you know who baked them?"

"Mrs. Smith. She's the one who owns Pumpkin," Sofia said.

"Your cookies are delicious, Mrs. Smith," Jason called out. Several people turned to stare at him, though not Mrs. Smith or Grampy, who were probably too deaf to hear him over the chatter of the fellowship hall. Jason whispered to Sofia, "Which one is Mrs. Smith?"

She laughed. "The woman speaking with Grampy."

"You must introduce me...I mean, us," he said, reaching for Mom's hand.

"I've met Mrs. Smith before." Mom shook her head and sighed, but she was smiling. "This isn't my *first* time at church."

"Yeah, it's her second," Sofia said.

Jason laughed. "You're a regular church lady."

Mom rolled her eyes. "I'm beginning to think you're a bad influence, Jason."

Jason brought his free hand to his mouth to cover his gasp. "Me? A bad influence? Who's the one who brought the family to church this morning? Now go introduce me to Mrs. Smith." He laced his fingers through Mom's, and, to Sofia's surprise, grasped Sofia's hand, too.

"Mrs. Smith," Jason repeated, louder this time.

She turned and smiled at Sofia. "I'm so pleased you've brought your mother to church this morning. And this handsome young man must be Jason."

Without releasing his grip on Sofia's hand, Jason took an exaggerated bow. "At your service, Ma'am." He straightened and added, "Your peanut butter and chocolate kiss cookies are legendary."

Mrs. Smith laughed. "I'm glad you like them."

Mom gave his hand a pat. "Jason is an amazing chef."

"He sure is," Grampy agreed.

"I'm not a chef." Jason's cheeks turned pink. "I just like to cook."

"A man who likes to cook. Sounds like a keeper to me." Mrs. Smith winked at Mom.

"He is," Mom said.

Sofia hoped she meant it. Jason was the best boyfriend Mom ever had. Including, it seemed, Sofia's own father.

"How's Pumpkin, dear?" Mrs. Smith asked. "I hope he's not giving you any trouble."

"He's doing great." She'd been caring for Mrs. Smith's cat for over six weeks, but always knew he'd be returning to Mrs. Smith's house after she recovered from her fall. Sofia hadn't expected to grow so attached to him. "He misses you, though." She wasn't sure if this was true or not, but it seemed like the right thing to say.

"I miss him, too." Mrs. Smith brushed her fingers through her sparse white hair. "My physical therapist promised that if I keep doing my exercises, I'll be ready to care for him in a few weeks. Do you think you could keep him for a bit longer while I get stronger?"

Sofia glanced at Grampy, who nodded. "I'd be happy to take care of Pumpkin as long as you need." That would give her more time to grow even more attached to the enormous orange tabby. Would Mom and Grampy let her get a cat of her own? Maybe Jason could help her talk them into it.

It was after two o'clock by the time Jess's truck and horse trailer pulled into Stephanie's driveway. Snickers and Kit Kat raced around their paddock, snorting, squealing, and bucking. Sundance hollered from inside the barn, where Sofia had left him to wait in his stall until it was time to tack him up for their trail ride.

Eager to help them unload Magic and Rosie, Sofia waved to Jess and Jason and hurried to the back of the trailer. She hopped up and down, glimpsing Magic's enormous rear end and Rosie's strawberry-colored tail.

Her coat pocket vibrated. *It better not be Olivia or Anika begging to ride Sundance.* She hadn't told them about her plan to ride with Jess and Jason this afternoon, *or* her decision to invite Gramma Lisa to Acadia. Maybe she should ignore the text. But what if it was important? Sighing, she retrieved the phone from her pocket.

It was Gramma Lisa! *Anna is happy to take care of Delilah for the weekend if you still want me to ride with you in Acadia National Park.*

Her fingers hovered over the screen, about to send an enthusiastic emoji, when she realized she hadn't asked Jess's permission. Jess wouldn't think Gramma Lisa was too old, would she? And what would Mom say? Mom and Gramma Lisa hadn't always gotten along. They'd forgiven each other—for now—but that didn't mean Mom would want to spend a weekend with her. Of course, Gramma Lisa would be riding most of the time, but Mom could be unpredictable when—

"Ready to unload the beasts?" Jason asked.

Startled, Sofia looked up from her phone and shoved it back into her coat pocket. "Oh! Yes."

Jess joined them. "Nice afternoon for a ride."

Sofia nodded. Should she ask Jess about Gramma Lisa now, or wait until after their trail ride?

Jason unlatched the trailer's door and swung it open while Jess entered through the side door near Rosie's head. Then he unhooked the bar behind the Appaloosa's rear end.

"Here she comes," Jess called out as Rosie took a step backward. Her hind leg pawed in the air for a moment, searching for solid ground before she stepped down and out of the trailer. The mare blinked and her nostrils widened, taking in the unfamiliar scents of Stephanie's barn.

Jess stepped out after Rosie. She rubbed her gloved fingers through her horse's sparse mane.

"Do you want to lead Magic out of the trailer?" Jason asked Sofia.

"Sure!" Sofia took the lead rope from Jason's outstretched hand, proud he trusted her to handle the massive half-Percheron. She walked around the side of the trailer, opened the side door, and greeted the black gelding with a pat on his thick neck. She clipped the lead rope onto his halter. "Ready?"

Sofia ducked under the chest bar as Magic stepped backward. He didn't need her guidance, so she simply followed him off the trailer.

"Thanks," Jason said when Sofia gave him his horse. He tied Magic to the side of the trailer. "We've already groomed them, so all we need to do is tack up."

Jess was already lifting a Western saddle onto Rosie's back.

Sofia sucked in a breath. She couldn't wait until after their ride to find out if Jess would allow Gramma Lisa to ride Magic. She needed to know now!

"Uh... Jess?"

Jess looked over her shoulder. "What? Is something wrong?"

Sofia shook her head. "I want to ask you something about our Acadia trip."

"Ask away." Jess turned back to her horse and reached under Rosie's belly for the girth.

The cinch, Sofia corrected herself. That's what a girth was called on a Western saddle.

She took a deep breath. "I wonder if my grandmother can ride instead of Olivia or Anika. Gramma Lisa is the one who gave me Sundance. She's got her own horse, but it would be a long drive from Connecticut, so I hoped she could ride Magic," Sofia said. "She's a good rider...and she's not that old," she quickly added, unsure of her grandmother's exact age. "Not old like Grampy."

"Of course, your grandmother can come," Jess said as she tightened Rosie's cinch. "And honestly, I feel a lot more comfortable about her joining us than Anika or Olivia. Jason shouldn't have promised you could bring a friend without consulting me first." She shot her brother a nasty glare.

Jason glared back. "I didn't promise anything. I just suggested it was a possibility."

"I thought..." Sofia looked away, heat creeping up her neck and spreading over her cheeks. She'd been so preoccupied by the decision of which friend to invite, she'd forgotten it wasn't really her choice in the first place. It had always been Jess's. "Thank you for allowing Gramma Lisa to ride with us."

Jason's eyebrows furrowed. "How does your mom feel about your grandmother coming on the trip?" he asked, his tone serious but gentle.

Sofia looked away, embarrassed to admit the truth. Would Jess withdraw her permission if she knew about Mom and Gramma Lisa's past conflicts? The weight of her worry pressed on her chest, making it hard to breathe.

"You haven't spoken with her about it yet?" He placed a reassuring hand over her shoulder. She looked up to meet his gaze, his kind, blue eyes full of empathy. Sofia shook her head and turned away again, overwhelmed by the prospect of Mom's disapproval.

"I understand." Jason placed his other hand over Sofia's shoulder, giving her a gentle squeeze. "You didn't want to say anything until you knew your grandmother could come. But you'll tell your mother after our ride."

She swallowed, anxiety gnawing at her stomach. Jason didn't understand how Mom could be, sometimes. Confronting her was almost worse than telling Olivia and Anika she wouldn't be taking them to Acadia. Sofia had to wait until Mom was in the right mood, and even if she was in a good frame of mind, she still might overreact.

She took a step back and Jason's hands fell to his sides. "I need to tack up Sundance," she said, and hurried to the barn.

"I'd forgotten about this trail," Jess said as they trotted up the slope along the edge of the hayfield. The short grass was still mostly green, but the maple trees bordering the field had lost most of their leaves, now scattered like a golden-brown carpet under their horses' hooves. Rosie led the way, followed by Magic.

Sofia struggled to prevent Sundance from galloping up the hill as he had when she'd ridden with Jason two weeks before. He tossed his head impatiently, straining against the bit. She hoped he wouldn't be this competitive on the carriage trails at Acadia.

"The turn into the woods is just ahead," Jason called out.

Jess slowed Rosie to a walk. "We went this way a few times when we were teens, remember? I rode Magic, and you rode your dirt bike."

"And you always wanted to race me, even though my dirt bike was faster." Jason chuckled.

Sofia kept a firm pressure on Sundance's reins, but instead of walking calmly behind Magic, he surged past his rival.

"Sundance might have beaten my dirt bike, though," Jason said.

"Sorry." Sofia worried Sundance would run right into Rosie's strawberry roan haunches, but he settled into a walk a few feet behind the mare's tail. Were they too close? "Does Rosie kick?"

"She might," Jess warned. "But she doesn't seem upset. Her ears aren't pinned back or anything."

They turned right into the woods. Sundance followed behind Jess and Rosie on a loose rein, just as he always had when riding with Delilah and Gramma Lisa. The palomino lowered his head and blew out a soft, contented sigh.

"Your horse really likes Rosie," Jason observed.

"Yeah, it's kind of weird." Sofia patted Sundance's neck. "He wanted to race ahead of Magic, but now he's totally calm."

"Maybe he's falling in love," Jason said.

Sofia wrinkled her nose. "That's gross."

"I don't know, Sofia," Jess said. "The Sassy Appy seems to like Sundance, too."

Sofia shook her head. It was bad enough for Ryan to have a crush on Anika. She didn't need her horse crushing on Rosie. Did horses even fall in love?

No, Sundance couldn't be in love, but maybe the Sassy Appy reminded him of Delilah. Tiny Snickers and Kit Kat were adorable, but nothing like Gramma Lisa's moody Morgan. And, for some reason, Sundance viewed the enormous Magic as more of a rival to compete against than a friend. But Rosie?

Maybe Sundance had found a genuine friend.

Chapter 16

"How was your ride yesterday?" Anika asked Sofia when she entered Mr. Barclay's homeroom. Their bug-eyed Language Arts teacher stood outside the door, chatting with the assistant principal, Mrs. Moore.

Sofia quirked an eyebrow. She hadn't told Anika she'd ridden with Jess and Jason, so how did she know? "Good. Sundance likes Rosie."

Anika had coated her lips in sparkly pink gloss this morning. "Maybe next time you go out, I can ride Magic. We should fit in some practice rides before Acadia."

"Maybe." Sofia settled into the desk in front of Anika's and closed her eyes. Her stomach twisted as she considered how to inform Anika that Gramma Lisa had taken her place. It hadn't seemed complicated last night when she'd rehearsed in front of her bedroom mirror, but the words refused to come now. They stubbornly clung to her churning insides, just as they had when she should have told Mom. Her mother had been in such a great mood after spending much of the day with Jason that Sofia hadn't wanted to break the spell.

"I told Ryan I'll help him get back on a horse," Anika said. "That way, he can take a turn riding with us. I'll walk next to him, so he doesn't get scared. We could try it out this afternoon."

Sofia stifled a groan and buried her face in her hands.

"What's wrong with that?" Anika sounded defensive. "He doesn't want to admit it to you, but falling off Sundance totally freaked him out."

Sofia turned in her seat to face Anika. "I know he's freaked out," she said more forcefully than she intended. Ben looked up at them from his seat at the back of the classroom, smirking.

Anika narrowed her eyes. Her lids shimmered with silver eyeshadow, instead of her usual gold. "Then why don't you want to help him?"

"I've tried! Every time Olivia and I bring it up, he makes an excuse. I know it's because he's scared, but what do you expect me to do? Force him?"

"The problem is Olivia." Anika crossed her arms over her chest. "I don't know why she's so mean to him."

"The problem," Sofia said, her cheeks blazing, "is that you guys keep telling me what to do! It's not your decision. It's my decision! Sundance is my horse, and the Acadia trip is supposed to be a family trip."

"Then why did you invite us to come?"

"I didn't invite you!" Sofia shouted. "You and Olivia invited yourselves."

"We did not!" Anika's voice rose in volume to match Sofia's.

Sofia gulped in a deep, shaky breath, attempting to calm herself as her classmates gaped at her. She glanced toward the door. Mr. Barclay and Mrs. Moore were still talking.

What would happen when the new kid picked a fight with the most popular girl in sixth grade? Nothing good. And once Sofia informed Anika that Gramma Lisa would be riding in their place, Olivia and Ryan might reject her, too.

She slowly exhaled, hoping to steady her voice. "Jess is the one who mentioned it to you, not me. Remember? Ever since then, you and Olivia have been trying to make me choose between you."

Anika pouted. "But we decided to take turns."

Sofia shook her head. "You and Olivia decided. Not me."

"Yeah, I guess that's true." Anika's shoulders slumped. "I'm sorry about that. It wasn't fair to you."

Anika hadn't reacted the way she'd expected. She'd even apologized for her behavior. "I asked my Gramma Lisa to come," Sofia said, her voice barely a whisper.

"So, she's bringing her Morgan mare," Anika said. "That still leaves Magic—"

"Gramma Lisa's going to ride Magic," Sofia interrupted before Anika could continue to make choices for her. "It's too far to bring Delilah."

"Oh." Anika sighed. Her head drooped so far it nearly rested against the hard surface of her desk.

Sofia chewed her lip to prevent herself from blurting out an apology. She was sorry, in a way. Not sorry she'd chosen Gramma Lisa instead of Anika, but sorry she'd disappointed her friend.

The buzzer sounded, and Mr. Barclay hurried into the room, his fleshy pale cheeks drooping from under his gray mustache. "Good morning, good morning. Settle down. It's time for the announcements," he intoned.

Sofia peeked over her shoulder at Anika.

Anika looked away.

When Sofia entered the noisy cafeteria, there were still two vacant seats at Anika's lunch table. Chloe waved to her, but Sofia shook her head.

"I'll sit with Olivia and Ryan," she said, grateful for an excuse to avoid Anika's continued disappointment in her. Anika hadn't been rude or mean during their morning classes together. The problem was, she hadn't uttered a single word to Sofia.

She found an empty table on the other side of the lunchroom and waited for the twins. Olivia joined her first.

"There's two spots at Anika's table," Olivia said. "If we hurry, we can sit there."

"I don't want to leave Ryan out." It wasn't a lie. Not exactly, anyway.

"That's considerate. Not that he deserves it." Olivia pulled out a chair and sat. She leaned her crutches against the table and unzipped her lunchbox. "Why does Mom keep putting pears in my lunch? She knows I don't like them. Do you want it?"

Sofia shook her head. Her stomach rumbled with hunger, but she wasn't at all sure she could keep food down. Olivia still didn't know she'd invited Gramma Lisa to Acadia. Did Ryan? Sofia had seen him talking with Anika in the hallway after Spanish class.

And there he was, pushing his way through a crowd of seventh-grade boys to join them at the table.

"What's wrong with Anika," Ryan demanded as he plopped into the empty chair beside Sofia. "She said I needed to talk with you about it."

"I uh..." Sofia swallowed.

"What did you say to her?" Ryan said, his tone accusatory.

Olivia took a bite of her egg salad sandwich, looking amused.

"It's just that..." Sofia took a deep breath. "I decided to invite Gramma Lisa to ride Magic during the Acadia trip."

Olivia's brow furrowed. "Instead of us?"

Sofia nodded.

"That's so mean," Ryan said. "No wonder she's upset."

Olivia glared at her brother. "Why is it mean?"

He threw his hands into the air. "Because we were going! Sofia uninvited us!"

Sofia sighed. "I didn't—"

"Yes, you did!" Ryan shouted. "And Anika promised she'd walk next to me when I rode."

"I don't remember anything about you riding," Olivia said.

"Anika told me last night. We were texting."

Olivia raised an eyebrow. "You text with Anika?"

Ryan pouted. "So, what if I do?"

Sofia rubbed her temples, wishing she could magically disappear. Or, better yet, go back in a time machine to the Sunday dinner at Jason's house, when Jess brought up the Acadia trip and Jason said Sofia could invite a friend. She should have said no. Instead, her three best friends now hated her.

"I'm sorry," Sofia whispered, fighting back tears. "I'm so, so sorry."

"You don't need to apologize," Olivia said. "We're the ones who should apologize. This is your trip. It isn't fair that we keep pressuring you to make it about us."

Ryan frowned. "But Anika was so excited about—"

"No." Olivia shook her head at her brother. "That's exactly what I'm talking about. Apparently, you and Anika have been making all these plans about riding, but did you even ask Sofia about it first?"

Ryan looked away.

"Did you?" Olivia demanded.

He shook his head.

"And Anika and I decided to take turns riding Magic. We never asked Sofia if that's what she really wanted." Olivia turned to Sofia. "Did we?"

"It's not that I didn't want to include you. It was just..." Sofia wrung her hands under the table. "It was just getting so complicated and...stressful."

"Olivia stresses me out, too," Ryan said.

"And you and Anika stress me out." Olivia rolled her eyes. "Just think how poor Sofia feels having to deal with all three of us."

You've got that right.

"I'm sorry we pressured you," Olivia said.

"I'm sorry, too," Ryan said.

Sofia's hands relaxed as the knot in her gut loosened. Ryan and Olivia didn't hate her, after all. But what about Anika? She glanced toward her table, but there were too many people in the way for her to get a clear view of her friend.

"Are you free after school?" Sofia asked the twins. "If Anika will come, she can help Ryan ride Sundance."

Ryan's eyes widened. "Really? You wouldn't mind?"

"It's about time you got back on a horse," Sofia said. "And Sundance is much calmer now that he's used to being at Stephanie's."

"What about me?" Olivia whined. "I want to ride, too!"

Sofia sighed. Nothing had changed.

Olivia grinned at her and punched her in the arm. "Just kidding!"

Chapter 17

By the time Anika's mom dropped her off at the barn, Sofia, Olivia, and Ryan had already finished cleaning the stalls and grooming and saddling Sundance. Sofia dismounted and led her horse to the gate, studying Anika's movements as she stepped out of the car with none of her usual bounce.

The leaves on Stephanie's huge maple tree trembled in the brisk wind. Some released their grip, raining a shower of whirling gold onto the picnic table where Grampy sat. He brushed one away from his shoulder and stood. "Good afternoon, Anika. Ryan tells me you're going to help him get back in the saddle."

Anika simply nodded, her hands hanging limply at her sides.

Sofia's shoulders sagged. Anika must still be angry with her. She probably only showed up to keep her promise to Ryan.

A leaf fluttered against Sundance's muzzle. He snorted and shook his head. Though he hadn't spooked during their warmup, his nostrils flared and his ears pricked forward, alert to the sights, sounds, and smells of the blustery fall afternoon. This might not be the best day for Ryan to overcome his fear of riding.

"Sundance is all ready for you," Olivia said. "Sofia had *lots* of time to warm him up while we waited for you to get here."

Anika frowned. "My mum—"

"Yeah. We know. Your mother always runs late." Olivia glanced at the darkening sky. "Let's get started. Ryan, are you ready?"

"I think so?" Ryan grimaced.

Anika wrapped an arm around his shoulder and gave it a squeeze. "You can do this. Sofia and I are going to be right with you. Nothing bad will happen."

Unless it does. Sofia tried to push the thought from her mind. She offered her riding helmet to Ryan, who was leaning heavily into Anika's embrace, as if he might crumple to the ground without her support.

"Do you need me to do anything?" Grampy asked.

Anika's arm dropped to her side as she took a step away from Ryan. "Thanks, Mr. Richardson, but you can sit down and rest. We should be all set."

Was it Sofia's imagination, or did Anika look sad? Not angry. Not annoyed. Just sad.

Ryan looked sad, too, but Sofia was pretty sure it was because Anika wasn't into cuddling with him this afternoon. With a frown, he buckled the helmet's chin strap under his throat. She hoped he wouldn't need it.

Olivia tugged her brother's coat sleeve. "Come on. Sofia's waiting."

He glanced at Anika before following Olivia through the paddock gate.

Anika sighed and followed, too.

Sofia re-checked Sundance's girth. The last thing they needed was for his saddle to slip while Ryan attempted to mount up. The palomino turned his head toward her shoulder, peering at her with large, brown eyes, as if to say, *"I thought we were already finished."*

She shook her head. *Nope. You've still got a job to do.*

"Do you think the stirrups will be the right length for him?" Anika asked. "Ryan's a bit taller than you."

Sofia tugged on the stirrup leather, sliding the strap down a few inches so she could undo the buckle. She lowered it by two holes, then repositioned it so the buckle wouldn't rub against Ryan's thigh. She was adjusting the other stirrup when Ryan asked, "How am I supposed to get on him?"

"The way you mounted up before, stupid," Olivia said.

Ryan groaned. "I mean, I don't think I can reach my leg up that high. Can I stand on the picnic table?"

"I'll give you a leg up," Anika offered.

"What's that?"

Anika cupped her hands together. "You just put your knee into my hands, and I'll help push you up into the saddle."

"Like they do with the jockeys before the Kentucky Derby?" Ryan asked, sounding unconvinced.

Olivia snorted. "You're a lot fatter than a jockey."

Ryan's cheeks flushed bright pink.

"That's not helping his confidence," Anika said. "Don't worry, Ryan. It will work. You've got to trust me."

Sofia closed her eyes, wishing Ryan would hurry and get on her horse. The sun had nearly disappeared behind the trees, and feeding time was in less than an hour. Snickers and Kit Kat were already waiting in their stalls. The longer Ryan took, the more likely Sundance would grow impatient.

"Ready?" Anika asked, just as Sundance lurched forward.

Sofia pulled on his reins to steady him.

"Uh...what if he goes crazy again?" Ryan's voice trembled.

"He won't," Anika promised.

Sofia wasn't so sure.

"Mom! Look! I'm riding!" Ryan shouted from Sundance's back as Pastor Amy got out of her van.

Sofia clutched Sundance's reins as he snorted and tossed his head. They'd already circled the paddock twice, with Sofia leading and Anika walking close to Ryan's side while he gripped the saddle with both hands.

Pastor Amy waved to Grampy as she approached the paddock fence. "Look at you, Ryan!"

"He's a regular cowboy," Grampy said.

Sofia glanced at Anika. Surely her horse-savvy friend recognized Sundance's body language even if Ryan, Grampy, and Pastor Amy did not. Olivia must have known, too, but for once she'd kept her opinions to herself.

Anika patted Ryan's thigh. "You're doing amazing, but since your mum's here and it's getting dark—"

"But I've only been riding for a few minutes! And I need to practice steering him."

"It's always best to end on a good note," Sofia said, remembering what Stephanie had taught her about horse training.

"Exactly," Anika said. "You've gotten over your fear of riding. That's a big accomplishment. You can practice steering next time."

"But last time..." Ryan bit his lip.

"Last time what?" Anika asked.

"Last time he tried to dismount, he fell off," Olivia said, apparently unable to remain silent. At least she didn't elaborate. Sofia was anxious enough about Sundance's nerves without being reminded of the frightening accident.

"Oh," Anika glanced at Sofia. "Don't worry. Sofia's going to hold Sundance nice and still. And I'm right here."

"Let's bring Sundance closer to the gate first," Sofia suggested as he tossed his head again. If Ryan lost his balance while dismounting at the far side of the paddock, Sundance could be more likely to bolt.

"Great idea," Anika said. "That way your mum can see you better. Maybe she can take your picture before you dismount."

"She can get a before and after shot." Olivia snickered.

"Not helpful, sis," Ryan squeaked.

A gust of icy wind sent a whirlwind of leaves swirling under Sundance's belly. He stepped sideways, his neck tense, nostrils flaring, and the whites of his eyes showing.

"Whoa. Easy, Sundance," Sofia whispered as she tightened her grip on his reins.

Ryan clutched the saddle, his eyes even wider than Sundance's. "What is he doing?"

"He's just a little jumpy because of the wind," Anika said. "Sofia has it under control."

Sofia hoped Anika was right. They were only half-way to the gate, and she wasn't confident she could prevent her jittery horse from spooking if another gust of wind blew leaves in their direction.

Ryan shivered. "He's not going to freak out again, is he?"

"Of course not," Anika said. "And I'm right here to catch you."

"I'd like to see you do that," Olivia said.

"We're almost there." Anika ignored Olivia's snicker.

"You're doing great, Ryan!" Pastor Amy called out. "Just a few more steps."

Sofia held her breath.

"See? You made it," Anika said as Sofia halted Sundance a few feet in front of the paddock gate. "Smile for your mum."

Pastor Amy snapped a few pictures with her phone. Sofia wondered if Ryan would look as anxious in the photos as she felt.

They shouldn't have taken Ryan out for a ride under these conditions. If something had gone wrong... No. She couldn't think about it yet, not before Ryan was safely on the ground. She glanced at Anika, silently communicating the need for continued caution.

Anika nodded almost imperceptibly. "Okay, Ryan. Time to dismount. Take it nice and slow."

"But what if—"

"You've got to trust us. Sofia's holding Sundance, and I'm right here." Anika tapped Ryan's foot. "Take both feet out of the stirrups. It's much safer that way. That's right. Now, lean forward a little bit and swing your right leg over the saddle."

"But what if it gets caught?" Ryan's voice quavered. "What if I lose my balance and I fall?"

"You can do it." Anika placed her hand on the small of Ryan's back. "I'm not tall enough to hold you while you get down, but if your leg gets caught on the saddle—which it won't—I promise I'll help you get it unstuck."

"Do you need me to help?" Grampy asked.

"No, Ryan can do this," Anika said. "He just needs to trust himself."

Sofia's heart pounded. She didn't dare to watch. How could Anika be so calm?

"Ready? One. Two. Three!"

Sofia gripped Sundance's reins so tightly her knuckles were probably turning white from under her gloves. Sundance didn't move.

"Umph." Ryan grunted as he slid from the saddle and landed heavily with both feet on the ground. "I did it! I did it!"

Sundance snorted at the sound of Ryan's enthusiastic pronouncement, but at least he didn't spook.

Ryan wrapped his arms around Anika's back and squeezed. Anika let out a sharp breath.

"Don't kill her," Olivia said.

"Sorry." Ryan stepped back, his face flushing.

Anika grinned at him. "See, riding isn't so scary, is it? You just need to learn how to relax and trust yourself."

Relax and trust yourself? Sofia's pulse pounded in her ears. They were lucky Ryan hadn't gotten dumped again. She never should have allowed Ryan to ride when Sundance was so tense and spooky. Instead of trusting herself, she'd allowed guilt over not inviting her friends to Acadia to push aside her better judgment.

Sundance pawed the ground and tossed his head. "We should bring him back to the barn, now," Sofia said.

"Just one more picture," Ryan insisted. "I want one with just me and Anika next to Sundance."

Sofia reluctantly handed her horse's reins to Anika. "It's getting close to feeding time."

Anika shrugged. "It will only take a few seconds."

Pastor Amy allowed Olivia and Ryan to follow Anika, Sofia, and Sundance to the barn, but after they untacked and put away the saddle, she insisted it was time to leave.

"But I want to groom him," Ryan complained.

Pastor Amy crossed her arms over her chest. "I've got a meeting tonight, and you've got homework to do."

Ryan handed Sofia the curry comb he'd just picked up and turned toward Anika, stretching out his arms. "Thanks for helping me," he said as he pulled her into a hug.

Olivia rolled her eyes. "You should thank Sofia, too."

"Thanks, Sofia. You're the best," he said on his way out of the barn without giving *her* a hug.

Sofia studied Anika's expression. She must have realized by now that Ryan had a crush on her. Did she like him back? Or was she just being nice?

Anika ran her hand along Sundance's back. He lowered his head and blew out a long, fluttery breath. Now that he was inside the barn with Snickers and Kit Kat, he looked like he was ready for a nap.

"You did an amazing job handling Sundance," Anika said. "He was so tense, but you kept him under control the entire time."

Sofia glanced toward the barn door. Grampy was waiting in the car with the heat running. Stephanie would be home any minute. "We were lucky. Ryan could have gotten hurt." She closed her eyes and rested the top of her head against Sundance's muzzle. His lips nuzzled her hair.

"But he didn't," Anika said. "Nothing bad happened."

Sofia looked up and rubbed slobber from her forehead. "But what if it had?"

Anika shrugged. "I thought the same thing, but I didn't want Ryan to get worried. And everything turned out okay, so there's nothing to get upset about now that it's over."

"I'm not upset..."

Anika sighed.

"What?"

"I *know* you're upset. You're not a very good actress, Sofia."

"Like you?" The thought leaped from Sofia's tongue before she could rein it in.

"Yeah. Like me."

Chapter 18

S ofia rubbed the curry comb in circles under Sundance's mane and down to his chest, afraid to make eye contact with Anika. She hadn't intended to accuse her friend of being an actress, yet instead of being defensive, Anika had readily admitted to being one. What had she meant?

Anika selected a dandy brush from Sundance's grooming tote and sighed. "I really wanted to ride with you at Acadia."

Sofia swallowed. Now that they were alone, Anika could finally give her the guilt trip she'd undoubtedly planned since this morning during school. That must be what she meant about being a good actress. She'd held back her feelings all day, and now they were about to be unleashed. "I'm sorry," Sofia muttered without looking up.

Anika flicked the brush over Sundance's back. "I'm glad you can go with your grandmother, though."

"Really?" Sofia paused her grooming of Sundance and risked a peek at Anika. "Aren't you mad at me?"

Anika shook her head. "I'm disappointed, but not mad." She returned her attention to Sundance, running the brush over the places where the saddle and girth had left indentations in his winter coat. Sundance shifted his weight onto his right side and cocked his left hind leg so the tip of his hoof rested on the floor.

"It's important to spend time with your grandmother while you still can," Anika said after a while. "I wish..."

Sofia waited for Anika to finish her thought, but her friend continued to brush Sundance. After another minute passed, Sofia asked, "What do you wish?"

Anika rubbed her eyes with the back of her hand. "I wish I had the chance to do stuff with my gran before she got cancer."

"Is she..." Sofia paused, afraid she might say the wrong thing. *Dead? Just sick?*

"She's on hospice," Anika said. "In India. My father is taking care of her."

"That's sad." Sofia was unsure exactly what *hospice* meant, but she'd heard the word enough times to realize Anika's grandmother must be dying.

"I haven't seen her in two years. I'm afraid I won't get to say goodbye." A sob escaped Anika's lips and she buried her face into Sundance's neck.

Not sure what else to do, Sofia patted Anika's back. "I'm sorry." Her words sounded feeble and inadequate.

"I begged Mum to let me visit her, but Mum doesn't want me to miss any school. She says I'll have to wait until Christmas vacation." Anika's shoulders shook. "What if it's too late by then?"

Sofia wanted to reassure her it wouldn't be too late, but how could she promise that? For all she knew, Anika's grandmother was gasping out her last breath at that very moment. Instead, she rested her hand on Anika's shoulder while her friend sobbed into Sundance's neck.

Sundance gently nuzzled Anika's back. Horses always knew exactly what to do.

"Don't forget we're heading over to Jason's for supper," Grampy announced a few minutes after they'd returned home from the barn.

"How could I forget?" Jason was a much better cook than Grampy, and ordering pizza or subs from Ray's Variety, where Mom worked, wasn't nearly as exciting as it had been a few weeks ago. "Mom's going to be jealous."

"Humph." Grampy's mustache twitched.

"What is Jason making tonight?" Her mouth watered in anticipation.

"He said it's a surprise."

"As long as it doesn't have Moxie in it." Sofia wrinkled her nose and laughed as she and Grampy repeated Jason's familiar joke. "Puts hair on your chest."

Sofia dashed into her bedroom to change out of her smelly horse clothes, not that Jason or Jess would mind if she wore them. She was pulling her hoodie over her head when her phone vibrated with a call. It couldn't be Daddy yet, and her friends always texted her first before calling. She struggled to untangle her hair from the folds of the hoodie, finally resorting to a yank that ripped out a few strands as the sweatshirt slipped free.

She dove for the phone as it vibrated on her desk.

"Gramma Lisa!" Sofia's pulse quickened. She hadn't spoken with Mom about inviting her grandmother yet.

"Hello, Sofia. I hope I'm not calling you in the middle of dinner. Or feeding Sundance."

"No, I'm just getting ready to go over to Jason's house."

"That's nice," Gramma Lisa said. "I look forward to meeting him soon. He sounds like a wonderful man."

"He is." Sofia stared at her reflection in the mirror. A large section of hair had come loose from her ponytail and now stuck out in a frizzy clump on the left side of her head.

"I'm really looking forward to our trip." Gramma Lisa said. "I assume we're staying at a motel somewhere around Bar Harbor?

Do you know if your mom has made a reservation for me? And you'll need to let me know where to meet on Friday, unless you would want me to come up on Thursday night instead."

"Uh..." Sofia bit her lip, unsure whether to admit Mom didn't know Gramma Lisa was coming.

"Is your mother around? Could you hand her the phone so we can work out the plans?"

"Mom's at work."

"She's not going to Jason's house with you?" Gramma Lisa sounded surprised.

"Jason's making dinner for me and Grampy."

"Oh, that's...nice of him." Gramma Lisa took a deep breath. "Could you please ask your mother to call me when she gets home from work?"

Sofia's heart pounded. "She doesn't come home from work until very late, and you'll need to wake up early to feed Delilah. I can find out the details from Jason tonight and text you back." She hoped this would be enough of an excuse to prevent Gramma Lisa from speaking with Mom before she talked with her first.

"Okay, dear. I hope you have a nice dinner. Talk with you soon."

"Bye." Sofia's hands shook slightly as she ended the call. What would Mom say when she discovered Gramma Lisa would join them on their trip to Acadia? And what would Jason say when he found out Sofia hadn't spoken with Mom about it yet? Maybe she should get the details about the hotel from Jess instead.

Grampy knocked on her door. "Almost ready?"

"Just a minute." Sofia opened the middle dresser drawer and rummaged through it in search of a clean sweatshirt. The only one not in the laundry hamper was a tattered green hoodie. She'd worn it under her coat on the first day she'd met Sundance, almost two years earlier. She smiled, remembering how it used to be her favorite. How long had it been since she'd worn it?

She pulled the sweatshirt over her head and tugged at the sleeves, which fell more than an inch above her wrists. Sighing, she took it off and tossed it onto the floor.

As she dug through the drawer looking for a top that fit, her fingers brushed against an envelope. The secret birthday card she'd received from Abuela! Though Mom now knew about her correspondence with the Ruiz side of her family, she'd never shown her Abuela's card, which she'd hidden under the clothing in her dresser.

She turned the blue envelope over in her hands before sliding out her grandmother's card.

Feliz Cumpleaños, Nieta. Abuela had told her that her husband, Abuelo, died from cancer. Since Sofia hadn't even known she had a grandfather, she was more curious than sad to learn about his death. But Anika? How awful to know your grandmother was dying from cancer, and you might never see her again. Sofia brushed her fingers over Abuela's loopy signature before returning the card to its hiding place.

What if Abuela got sick? Or Grampy? Or Gramma Lisa?

Sofia lifted the worn green sweatshirt from the floor and cradled it against her chest, a flood of memories rushing through her mind. With a deep breath, she put it on and stared at her reflection in the mirror. She attempted to smooth out her hair, but realized it was a hopeless cause and reached for Grampy's old Red Sox baseball cap, instead.

"Ready." She stepped into the hallway to join Grampy.

Without waiting for Grampy, Sofia hurried from his Subaru and bounded up the four wooden steps leading to Jason's front door. The two pumpkins she and Jason had carved the night before greeted her with candles flickering behind their goofy, lopsided grins. As she raised her fist to knock, the door swung open.

Jason peered out into the darkness. "Where's Mr. Richardson?"

Sofia glanced over her shoulder. "He's still getting out of the car." She slipped past Jason and entered the house, her nostrils taking in the aroma of baking bread, garlic, butter, and something else she couldn't identify. "What's for dinner?"

Jason laughed. "You're worse than your Grampy. You can wait a few minutes to find out." He stepped through the door and onto the steps. "Mr. Richardson? Do you need any help?"

"Help?" Sofia heard Grampy's loud snort from inside Jason's living room. "I'm not a feeble old man yet."

"Of course not, Mr. Richardson."

Grampy entered the house and took a deep breath. "Whatever it is you've made, it smells delicious."

"That's because it *is* delicious." Jason winked at Sofia. "It will put hair—"

"On your chest!" Sofia giggled as she completed Jason's joke.

Jason shrugged. "It's true."

"Do you think Jess needs help with the animals?" Sofia hoped her question sounded innocent. Helping would give her an opportunity to ask Jess about the arrangements for their Acadia trip in private.

"They're all fed and tucked in for the night," Jason said.

"Oh."

"You sound disappointed." Jason put his hand on Sofia's shoulder. "You wanted to visit Rosie and Magic, didn't you?"

She nodded. Her cheeks flushed. It wasn't really a lie, was it? She enjoyed seeing the horses. And Tootsie and the goats. "Is Jess coming for dinner?"

"Are you kidding? Garlic butter pasta with chicken is her favorite meal."

Grampy closed his eyes and sniffed. "So, that's what you're making!"

"With homemade rolls." Jason grinned. "And Jess is bringing over an apple pie."

"Mmm..." The corners of Grampy's lips twitched under his mustache. "When can I move in with you?"

"Anytime, Mr. Richardson. Anytime." He patted Sofia's shoulder. "As long as Sofia moves in with me, too."

Was Jason just teasing? Or had he really invited them to live with him?

Jason and Mom had been together for less than two months. He must have been joking around. Besides, there weren't enough rooms in his house for all of them, unless she and Mom shared a bedroom. Sofia's face flushed as she realized that Jason, not her, would be the one sharing a room with Mom. If Grampy took over Jason's tidy study and she moved into the small bedroom...

But Grampy had his own house. And if Sofia lived with Jason, she wouldn't be able to ride her bike to Stephanie's house to care for Sundance, Snickers, and Kit Kat.

If I lived here, I could walk across the street to Jess's place. Sundance could share the pasture with Magic and Rosie, and there was plenty of room for another horse inside the spacious barn.

Sofia glanced at Jason, who was removing the tray of homemade rolls from the oven. He placed them into a small wicker basket like the one Gramma Lisa used to serve bread on special occasions. If they lived with Jason, would he prepare fancy dinners like this every night? Or was he just trying to impress them?

When Jason caught Sofia's gaze, he grinned and wiggled his eyebrows. "Prepare yourself to be amazed," he said. "These are the best rolls you'll ever taste."

"The best?" Sofia grinned back.

Jason nodded. "Only the best for my Sofia."

Chapter 19

S ofia was arranging forks, spoons, and knives around the dinner plates when Jess strode through the door, followed by Einstein and Harriet. Einstein raced across the room toward Jason.

He waved his arms at the big yellow dog. "Shoo. I'm not giving away handouts tonight."

"It never hurts to ask," Jess said. She placed a round, tin-foil-wrapped object on the kitchen counter next to the basket of dinner rolls. Sofia assumed it must be the promised apple pie.

Harriet danced around Sofia's legs. She attempted to ignore the Boston Terrier, but after Harriet hurled herself against Sofia's knee, she bent to pat the dog behind her ears.

"Don't give her any ideas," Jason said. "The last thing we need are two beggars under the table."

"They aren't *that* bad," Jess protested.

Jason shook his head, frowning. "Yes, they are. And I don't want them bothering Mr. Richardson."

Grampy shrugged. "I don't mind dogs."

"Stop it!" Jason grabbed Einstein by the collar just as the dog's front paws touched the edge of the kitchen counter. The yellow lab lurched forward and snatched a roll from the basket before Jason dragged him away. "This is why I don't want your dogs in my house when I have guests over."

So, we're just guests, after all. Jason must have been joking about them moving into his house. Sofia's shoulders sagged. What had she expected? Jason was just one of a long string of Mom's boyfriends. Eventually, Mom would get mad at him. They'd fight and break up, but hopefully not before their trip to Acadia.

"Sorry," Jess said. "I'll take them home."

"Can I come with you?" Sofia asked. This might be the only opportunity she'd have to speak with Jess in private.

"Sure, though I'm just going to run across the street, then come right back."

When Jess whistled, Harriet trotted to her side. Einstein hesitated, giving a hopeful glance at the basket of rolls before reluctantly joining them. Sofia grabbed her coat from where she'd tossed it onto Jason's sofa and hurried after Jess, who was already heading out through the door.

"Can I ask you something about our trip to Acadia?" Sofia asked after they'd crossed the street and were heading down Jess's long driveway.

"Ask away."

"I know the horses will be stabled at your friend's place, but where are we going to sleep?"

Jess slowed her pace and turned toward her. It was difficult to see her facial expression in the darkness, but Sofia worried Jess was looking at her with a puzzled expression. "Allison and I are staying with her cousin so we can look after the horses. I'm pretty sure Jason booked a room for you and your mother at the Sunrise Motel. He's planning to bunk with your great-grandfather. Are you worried about your grandmother? Do you think she'll want her own room, or will she share a room with you and your mom?"

"I'm not sure," Sofia said, though she was certain of the answer. Mom would not want to share a motel room with Gramma Lisa. Though they'd reconciled a few months earlier, their relationship remained cool and distant. Just because they'd forgiven each other didn't mean they trusted each other.

Mom put down her fork and placed her hand over Jason's.

Had Grampy said something wrong?

After a long pause, Jess finally spoke. But instead of explaining why she and Jason had suddenly grown solemn, she said, "Sofia wants to know about the motel arrangements for her grandmother. Did you book a separate room for her?"

Sofia's eyes widened. No! She shook her head at Jess, but it was too late.

Mom cocked her head in Sofia's direction. "What do you mean, book a room?"

Jason pursed his lips. "You haven't talked with her yet?"

Mom jerked her head back to face Jason. "Talked to me about what?"

"Sofia?" Jason stared at Sofia, his expression serious, though not unkind.

She looked away.

"Sofia?" Mom demanded.

"I, uh..." Sofia closed her eyes and swallowed back the sob that threatened to bubble up from her chest. "I invited Gramma Lisa to ride with us at Acadia, instead of Olivia or Anika."

"And you knew about this, Jason?" Mom snapped.

"Only since yesterday afternoon."

Sofia ventured a quick glance at Jason, who sucked in his lower lip.

"And you didn't think to mention it to me?" Mom's voice rose in pitch. "What about you, Grampy? Were you in on this little secret, too?"

Grampy shook his head and frowned. "This is the first I've heard about it."

Sofia gritted her teeth. It wasn't fair for Mom to blame Jason or Grampy. She sat straighter in her chair. "I was going to tell you, Mom. I just hadn't had the chance yet. I planned to talk to you after you got home from—"

"You were with me all day yesterday!" Mom crossed her arms over her chest. "You couldn't find a single extra moment to talk with me? Not to mention the fact that you should have asked my permission before inviting her first."

"You were okay with me bringing a friend," Sofia shot back, the fear of being yelled at replaced with defiance. If Mom had truly forgiven Gramma Lisa instead of clinging on to her ridiculous grudge, none of this would have happened. "So what if the friend I picked was Gramma Lisa?"

"You know what!" Mom glared at Sofia.

Jason rested his hand on Mom's shoulder. "It's going to be okay, Mandi. You and I are going to spend most of our time together in Bar Harbor while they ride."

Mom shifted her shoulders away from Jason's touch. "You, of all people, should understand about things like this."

"I do," he said, "which is why I think it's important to support Sofia's choice."

Mom's mouth gaped. "What are you implying?"

"I'm not implying anything." Jason's voice softened. "Only that we don't have to repeat the mistakes of our parents."

"You think I'm making mistakes?"

The knot forming in Sofia's gut twisted and tightened. She'd expected Mom to express displeasure with her decision to invite Gramma Lisa, but hadn't anticipated that her choice might cause trouble between Mom and Jason.

Grampy shifted uneasily in his chair. "I'm sure that's not what Jason is saying."

"Then what *is* he saying?" Mom scowled at Jason.

Jess glared at Mom. "Whatever messed up stuff happened between you and your mother has nothing to do with Sofia. And it's unfair to punish her for wanting a relationship with her grandmother."

"I'm not punishing her—"

"Really?" Jess pushed her chair out and stood, her freckled face blazing. "Why do you suppose she didn't want to tell you? Why do you think she spoke with me and Jason about it, rather than you?"

Sofia grabbed Mom's arm, but she jerked it away and rose to her feet. "This is none of your business," she shouted at Jess.

"Mom!" Sofia tried to drag her mother back to her seat. "It's not Jess or Jason's fault. I should have told you—"

"Yes, you should have." Mom broke free from Sofia's grasp and stomped from the kitchen. Without a word, she grabbed her coat and hurried out of the house, slamming the door behind her.

Sofia's eyes filled with tears. She'd ruined everything.

Jason stared at the place Mom had been sitting only a moment before, his face pale and eyes wide. Then his gaze turned to rest on Sofia. "I'm sorry," he said, his voice scratchy and barely above a whisper.

Sofia looked away, tears already spilling down her cheeks. Mom and Jason were breaking up. Their trip to ride in Acadia National Park would be canceled. She'd have to call Gramma Lisa and tell her not to come.

Family trip? It had been foolish for her to have believed, even for the briefest of moments, that she might become part of Jason and Jess's family.

Grampy cleared his throat. "I suppose Sofia and I ought to be going. Thank you for the meal and for your...uh...hospitality." He pushed his chair back from the table and leaned forward to stand.

Sofia rubbed her fists over her wet face. This was it. They were leaving and never coming back. She'd never see Jason or Jess or Magic or Rosie again. She'd never hear Tootsie's ear-splitting brays, or Einstein's booming barks, or Harriet's excited yips. All because she'd chosen to invite Gramma Lisa to ride with her instead of Olivia or Anika.

No. Because she'd hidden her choice from Mom.

Grampy got to his feet.

Jason stood, too. "Mr. Richardson, you don't need to go. You and Sofia are welcome to stay."

Grampy shook his head. "We'd better be—"

"What the heck are you doing, Jason?" Jess threw her hands into the air. "Don't just stand here! Go after her!"

Chapter 20

Sofia lay on her back with her blanket pulled up to her chin, staring into the darkness. If she gazed at a spot above the desk in her bedroom long enough, she could make out a faint patch of light cast by the rising moon.

Mom hadn't returned home.

Was she with Jason? If she was, that would be a good sign, right? If they'd broken up, surely Mom would be home by now...unless she'd gone somewhere to be alone.

Or she's already met someone else.

Sofia squeezed her eyes shut so forcefully bright sparkles of light flashed behind her eyelids. This was her fault. If she'd chosen Anika or Olivia instead of Gramma Lisa, Mom wouldn't have gotten angry with Jason. She would have enjoyed another slice of Jess's apple pie, and they would have hung out together *as a family.*

She flipped to her side and pulled the blanket over her head, remembering something else she'd hidden from Mom. How would she react if she discovered Sofia had called Daddy and Daniella from Jason's spare bedroom? It wasn't as if Mom had forbidden her to talk with them on the phone, but Mom had freaked out just because Jason had known about Gramma Lisa before she had. Sofia had to tell Mom about the video chat before she found out from someone else.

A gentle tap on the door startled Sofia awake.

She flung off her blanket and sat bolt upright. "Mom?"

Light from the hallway crept across the floor as the door opened a few inches.

"Mom?" she said, her voice louder this time.

"You're awake?" Mom asked as she slipped through the doorway and closed it behind her.

"Yes." Sofia swung her legs over the side of her bed and perched on the edge,

Mom padded across the room and sat beside her. "I know it's late, but I wanted to speak with you."

Sofia's heart hammered so forcefully it felt like it might leap out through her throat.

"I... I need to apologize to you." Mom's fingers brushed against the top of Sofia's hand.

You do? Sofia swallowed. "It was my fault. I should have told—"

"No. It wasn't your fault. I overreacted. I understand why you were reluctant to talk with me about inviting your grandmother." Mom squeezed Sofia's hand. "Jason is right. Gramma Lisa and I have had our problems, but it's not fair to get upset with you for wanting her to come on our trip. She's an important part of your life. And I'm sure she and I will get along just fine for a few days."

Sofia wrapped her arms around Mom's shoulders and buried her face against her warm chest. "Thanks for understanding."

Mom kissed the top of her head. "You should thank Jason, too."

Sofia smiled. They hadn't broken up after all. "I really like Jason," she said.

"Me, too." Mom leaned back and shifted on the bed like she was about to stand up. "It's a school night. You need your sleep."

Sofia took a deep breath. "I have to tell you something first."

Mom settled back beside her.

"I talked with Daddy and Daniella last week."

"Oh?"

"I made a video call." Sofia took another deep breath before continuing. "Jason let me use the internet at his house. I should have told you."

Mom nodded. "Thanks for letting me know."

It was difficult to read Mom's expression in the dark. Was she upset? "Mom?"

"Yes?"

"I love you."

Mom touched Sofia's cheek. "I love you, too, Honey Bear." She stood. "Now, get some sleep."

Chapter 21

Sofia wrapped her arms around her chest and shivered. Though the November afternoon was bright, a stiff wind pierced through her lightweight jacket and the sweatshirt she wore underneath. She'd already packed her warmer jacket and gloves into the suitcase she'd bring on her trip to Acadia the next morning. When she'd returned home from school, she considered taking them out to wear to the barn, but feared that with the excitement of getting Sundance ready and Gramma Lisa's upcoming arrival, she might forget to repack them. Better to freeze for an hour this afternoon than to be miserable during three days of riding.

She inspected Snickers and Kit Kat's half-empty water bucket. No ice.

Yet.

Some girls at Anika's lunch table had claimed they'd be getting the first snowfall of the season tonight. Chloe insisted she'd heard it on the TV weather report. "Up to three inches!"

Sofia had ridden in snow plenty of times with Gramma Lisa, but would Jess's friend, Allison, feel comfortable hauling a four-horse trailer in bad weather? What if they skidded off the road?

She looked up when she heard tires crunching over the loose gravel on Stephanie's driveway. Blinded by the sun, which was already low in the sky despite being only three-thirty in the after-noon, she shielded her eyes and squinted at the Murphy's van.

Ryan jumped out first, followed by Anika and Olivia.

Sofia smiled as she jogged toward the driveway to meet them. Asking Pastor Amy to bring Anika had been Olivia's idea. "That way, she can't blame her mom for making her late," she'd explained. "And she'll have to help with the chores for a change."

Ryan waved to Grampy, who was probably napping in his car. "It's so cold!" he called out to Sofia. "I heard it's going to snow. We might get six inches!"

"We're not going to get six inches," Olivia shouted back.

"Chloe said three," Anika said.

Olivia shook her head. "That's all hype. Our area is only sup-posed to get an inch at most. It will melt by mid-morning. And the weekend is going to be beautiful. The forecast for Acadia is sunny with highs in the mid-fifties. Perfect for riding."

Sofia sighed in relief.

"Now, let's get started on these chores," Olivia ordered. "Ryan, you muck out Snickers and Kit Kat's stalls. Anika, you can do Sundance's. Sofia needs to pack what Sundance will need for the trip."

Ryan put his hands on his hips and glared at his sister. "What are *you* doing, then?"

She grinned. "I'm organizing the packing list."

"Why can't I do that, and you muck out the stalls?" Ryan whined.

Olivia rolled her eyes. "Seriously, Ryan? You? Organize any-thing? We've all seen what your bedroom looks like."

Sofia snickered.

"I haven't," Anika said, looking amused.

"Believe me, you don't want to," Olivia said. "Now, let's get started. Sofia, you're going to need to measure out his grain rations for four feedings, and maybe a fifth one, just in case you stay later than expected on Sunday. I brought some resealable bags..."

Sofia prodded the mashed potatoes on her dinner plate, creating ridge marks with her fork.

"What's wrong?" Grampy asked. "You usually like my mashed potatoes. Has Jason's gourmet cooking spoiled you?"

She shook her head. "I'm just kind of nervous." Olivia had gone over every item Sofia and Sundance would need for their trip, and her suitcase was packed and ready. So why did her stomach feel like a washing machine spinning and churning the bits of pork chop, broccoli, and potatoes she'd forced herself to swallow?

Sundance's things were packed, but was her horse prepared for the trip? He was still settling into his routine at Stephanie's barn. Would he think Sofia was moving him away from Snickers and Kit Kat? What if he grew spooky and nervous again?

I'm a good rider. I can handle him.

But what if she couldn't? She'd only taken him out on the trail a few times over the past two months. Sundance enjoyed riding beside Rosie, but treated Magic more like a competitor to race. Would he respond differently when Gramma Lisa rode Magic instead of Jason? And then there was Thor, a horse neither Sundance nor Sofia had met. Jason had described him as a *monster Thoroughbred* who'd once attempted to bite him. Had Thor calmed down, or was he still a monster? If he tried to bite Jason, what would stop him from attacking Sundance? Why hadn't she thought about any of this before?

Grampy speared a second pork chop and transferred it to his plate. "What are you worried about? The trip? Or your mom and Gramma Lisa?"

Sofia sighed. *Thanks for reminding me of even more things to worry about.*

"I'm not sure Sundance is ready for the trip," she admitted.

"I'm sure he'll do fine." Grampy cut the meat into pieces. "Jess and your grandmother are experienced horsewomen. They'll know how to handle any problems, not that there'll be any." He paused, glancing at Sofia before popping a generously sized piece of pork into his mouth.

She nodded, not wanting to contradict Grampy's optimism. Gramma Lisa and Jess knew a lot about horses, but that didn't mean things couldn't go wrong.

At the sound of the doorbell, Sofia leaped to her feet and sprinted across the kitchen. "Gramma Lisa is here!" She flung open the door and grabbed Gramma Lisa around her middle.

"Goodness, Sofia," Gramma Lisa said, laughing. "You almost knocked me over!"

Sofia dropped her hands to her sides and jumped back. "Sorry!"

"Come here, my sweet, dear child." Gramma Lisa held out her arms and pulled Sofia back into a hug. "I've missed you so much."

Sofia buried her face into Gramma Lisa's squishy chest, breathing in her comforting lavender scent. "I'm so glad you're here."

"Thank you for inviting me to join you on this grand adventure." Gramma Lisa nuzzled the top of Sofia's head with her chin before planting a kiss on her forehead.

Sofia's shoulders relaxed. Grampy was right. She didn't need to worry about what might go wrong on their trip. No matter what happened, Gramma Lisa would take care of her and Sundance, just as she had done during so many trail rides before.

"Were you two raised in a barn?" Grampy squeezed past them and pulled the door shut. "It's good to see you again, Lisa. Would you like something to eat? I can't offer you a gourmet dinner like Mandi's boyfriend makes, but we've got some mashed potatoes and pork chops."

"Don't forget the broccoli," Sofia said as she released Gramma Lisa from her embrace.

"It puts hair on your chest," Grampy said, winking at Sofia.

"What?" Gramma Lisa wrinkled her nose.

Sofia grinned at Grampy. "It's just something Jason says whenever he wants me to try something new. Or healthy. Or disgusting, like this drink called Moxie." She laughed.

"Moxie?" Gramma Lisa shook her head, smiling. "You couldn't pay me enough to drink that vile stuff. Jason sounds like quite a character. I'm looking forward to meeting him."

"You're going to love him," Sofia said. "He's nothing like Patrick or Paul or…"

Gramma Lisa quirked an eyebrow.

Sofia's cheeks grew hot. As far as she knew, Gramma Lisa had never approved of any of Mom's boyfriends, not even Sofia's father. What if she disliked Jason, too? "Do you want me to get anything from your truck? You should sleep in my bed tonight. I'll take the couch."

"That can wait a few minutes," Grampy said, appearing confused by the sudden shift in Sofia's mood. "We're in the middle of dinner, and I'm sure Lisa would appreciate something to eat or drink after her long drive."

"Thank you. I'd love to join you for dinner." Gramma Lisa glanced at Sofia, who offered her grandmother what she hoped looked more like a genuine smile than a grimace. Why was it so important for Gramma Lisa to approve of Jason? It wasn't as if they'd spend any time together after the Acadia trip.

Because he's part of my family now.

More than Daddy and Daniella, her own father and stepmother? Weren't they her *real* family? Yet they were little more than strangers she'd exchanged a handful of letters with, and only met once on a video call. They didn't feel *real*. Not like Jason.

It was still dark when the piercing bleep from Sofia's alarm clock jarred her awake and sent her catapulting from the couch. Heart racing, she snatched it from the coffee table and switched it off before it woke the others. Stephanie had given her the clock back in June, after she'd overslept on the first morning she was supposed to feed Snickers and Kit Kat. Sofia had stopped using it after Grampy purchased a cell phone for her birthday. She'd forgotten how obnoxiously loud it was.

She sat on the edge of the couch and rubbed her stiff neck. So much for getting a good night's rest before the big trip. Hopefully Gramma Lisa slept comfortably in Sofia's bed.

Last night, it had seemed a good idea to set the alarm for 4:45. She'd have to feed Sundance early to allow him plenty of time to digest his grain before she loaded him onto the trailer for their three-and-a-half-hour drive. But now, as she yawned and stretched in the pitch-dark living room, she wondered what she'd do for the next hour before Gramma Lisa would accompany her to the barn.

She wandered over to the window and peered through the glass. Was it snowing? She switched on the porch light and opened the door. Swirling, fat snowflakes glittered as they danced to the ground. She slipped on her barn boots and stepped outside.

Wet flakes tumbled into her hair and melted on her outstretched hands.

On any other morning, it would be beautiful, but today? She sighed. At least Ryan had been wrong about the six inches part. Only a thin, white coating clung to the ground.

"What are you doing out here in your pajamas?"

Startled, Sofia whipped around to face Gramma Lisa. "It's snowing," she said.

"I can see that." Gramma Lisa smiled and stepped outside to join her on the porch steps. "The snow's quite pretty. It's also cold. You should put on your coat and close the front door unless you want Grampy to accuse you of being raised in a barn."

"He's not awake yet." Sofia forced a smile.

Gramma Lisa put an arm around Sofia's shoulders. "I can tell something's worrying you. Let's go inside and warm up. I'll make us hot chocolate and we'll talk."

By the time Sofia and Gramma Lisa arrived at the barn, the snow had stopped falling and the orangey-red glow of pre-dawn brushed the horizon. Snickers and Kit Kat's high-pitched whinnies and Sundance's rumbly nickers announced their presence as they stepped out of the truck. Though human-made clocks claimed breakfast was still a half-hour away, the horses didn't accept the premise of the end of Daylight Saving Time. With the clocks turned back an hour a few days before, the horses believed Sofia was delivering their meal thirty minutes late.

"We're coming!" Sofia called out as her boots crunched over the thin layer of snow. One of the horses, most likely Snickers, banged a hoof against a stall door.

"They're worse than Delilah," Gramma Lisa said.

"That's because there are three of them." Sofia grunted as she opened the heavy barn door. "No one is worse than Miss Piggy." She smiled, remembering Gramma Lisa's nickname for her food-obsessed Morgan mare.

The chorus of impatient equines rose several decibels as they entered the barn. Sofia hurried to the empty stall where Stephanie kept the grain and a few bales of hay. She scooped out Snickers' meager portion and handed it to Gramma Lisa. "You can give this to Snickers. He's the bay pinto with the blue eyes."

"The loud one. You can't tell me he's not Miss Piggy's equal," Gramma Lisa said.

"You're probably right," Sofia conceded. "That's why I feed him first."

Gramma Lisa returned a minute later to receive Kit Kat's feed bowl. "The little guy practically inhaled his breakfast. He might have set a world record."

Sofia chuckled as she scooped out Sundance's much bigger portion. He pawed and nickered impatiently as she walked across the aisle and opened his stall door. When she placed the large rubber feed bowl on the floor, he buried his face into the grain. She stayed inside his stall for a moment, watching as he gobbled up his breakfast.

"We're going on a trip," she whispered to him. "Jess and her friend are coming in a couple of hours to pick you up. Don't worry, though. It's just for the weekend. Magic and Rosie will be there, too. Gramma Lisa says you're going to do fine."

Sundance didn't look up until he finished his breakfast and flipped his feed bowl upside down. He peered at her through large brown eyes. A smattering of wood shavings from his stall bedding clung to his long, white forelock.

Sofia brushed her fingers over his thick golden coat and pulled a stalk of hay from his mane. She needed to begin the other morning chores. With Gramma Lisa's help, there'd be time to groom Sundance and return home to eat breakfast and pack their things into Gramma Lisa's truck before Jess and Allison arrived.

She wrapped her arms around Sundance's neck and breathed in his horsey scent. There was nothing to worry about. Her horse trusted her, and she trusted Gramma Lisa and Jess. They were about to go on the adventure of a lifetime.

Jess and Allison arrived fifteen minutes later than promised, giving Sofia enough time to get nervous all over again. At least most of the snow had melted. Only a few clumps of white clung to a shady area beside the barn and a few patches coated the grass under the trees at the top of Sundance's hilly pasture. Snickers and Kit Kat galloped around their paddock, bucking and neighing as Allison and Jess parked the four-horse trailer.

"I'd better get Sundance," Sofia said when her horse answered his friends' calls with frantic whinnies of his own. She hurried back into the barn to find him pacing in front of his stall door, his eyes wide and neck muscles tense.

She took a steadying breath. "You're going to be fine," she said to Sundance, though she needed the reassuring words as much as he did. She glanced over her shoulder as Gramma Lisa entered the barn behind her.

"He looks nervous. Do you want me to handle him?"

Sofia frowned and shook her head. Gramma Lisa probably meant well, but Sundance was *her* horse. She'd trained him and he trusted her.

She gripped his halter and lead rope and entered the stall. "You're going to be fine," she repeated, more confidently this time, and slipped the halter around his nose and over his ears. "It's time to go to Acadia National Park."

Sundance followed as she led him from his stall, down the barn aisle, and out through the door. He snorted and froze when he saw the trailer parked beside the gate to his pasture.

Jess waved at her from the driveway. Beside her stood a petite woman with shoulder-length, curly brown hair. She wore black paddock boots, fawn-colored riding breeches, and a navy-blue jacket with a logo of a jumping horse and the words, *Prestige Peak Stables* embroidered over the left side of her chest. "This is my friend, Allison," Jess said.

Gramma Lisa stepped forward. "I'm Lisa. Thank you for letting me join you on your trip."

Judging from the large quantity of hay tangled in her disheveled red locks, Jess hadn't brushed her hair for a while. Either that or she'd gotten into an argument with a bale of hay. Maybe both.

Jess smiled. "You're welcome."

"And this is my granddaughter, Sofia." Gramma Lisa held out her hand to Allison.

Allison gave Gramma Lisa's hand a quick shake, but her gaze remained focused on Sofia and Sundance. "Let's load him quickly before my horse gets worked up."

Jess smirked behind Allison's back.

A horse inside the trailer let out an ear-piercing whinny, followed by a loud bang that rocked the trailer.

"Thor!" Allison yelled. "Cut that out!"

Sundance's head shot up and he stepped backward. Sofia tightened her grip on his lead rope. "Easy, boy."

"Maybe I should take him from you," Gramma Lisa said.

Sofia gritted her teeth. "I can handle him." She'd forgotten how much of a worrier Gramma Lisa could be. Gramma Lisa had made all the decisions about what was safe or not safe for Sofia to do around horses. She hadn't even allowed her to enter Sundance or Delilah's stalls with their grain at breakfast time. "I'm not a beginner anymore," Sofia muttered.

She took a deep breath, willing herself to relax. Sundance trusted her. She needed to be a confident leader, to communicate that entering an unfamiliar horse trailer occupied by a *monster Thoroughbred* who was screaming his head off was a perfectly safe thing to do. She lifted her chin and stepped forward, hoping Sundance would follow.

Though Sofia was familiar with the design of most two-horse trailers, Allison's four-horse slant-loading trailer looked completely different. This trailer didn't have a ramp. Sundance would have to step up and sideways into the narrow space beside Rosie, who stood behind a partition made from metal tubes. Sofia bit her lip, considering the best approach.

Allison glanced inside the trailer, then back at Sofia. *"Hurry up and get your horse into the trailer before my precious Thor falls to pieces."* Allison didn't say these words out loud, but her sour, anxious expression made it perfectly clear that was what she was thinking.

"Come on, boy." Sofia led her horse to the edge of the trailer.

Sundance's nostrils widened and quivered. Did he smell Rosie?

"That's right. Your friend, Rosie, will be right beside you the whole way." Sofia stepped up into the trailer.

After a moment of hesitation, Sundance did, too.

Sofia smiled and gave his neck a pat. "Have fun with Rosie. I'll see you in a few hours."

Chapter 23

S ofia's heart pounded when she spotted the dark brown sign marking the entrance to Wildwood Stables. "We're finally here!"

Gramma Lisa sipped the coffee she'd purchased when they'd stopped for lunch in Ellsworth. It must have been cold by now. "Good thing," she said. "I really need to pee."

In front of them, the horse trailer turned right down the road leading to the park's stable, now closed for the season. Jess had explained that during the warmer months, equestrians could rent stalls to stable their horses, or even camp out with them. Teams of draft horses would pull wagonloads of tourists along the carriage roads leading up and down Day Mountain, the same route their group would ride this afternoon.

Sofia's eyes widened as several long, airy, shed-row style stables came into view, behind neat paddocks enclosed by split-rail wooden fencing. "Look at all those barns!"

Ahead was the main barn, a huge, white building with a wide-open door. What must be Day Mountain rose behind it. She wasn't sure she'd describe it as a mountain, exactly—more like an impressive hill—set against a spectacular blue sky. Much of the foliage had already fallen from the trees, but shades of gold and rust stood out against the dark green needles of pine, spruce, and fir, along with a scattering of bare white birch trees.

Allison parked her trailer along the side of the road, behind a smaller two-horse trailer with the words *Caution, Horses Aboard* printed in huge black letters. Several other trucks and trailers were parked along the main road and in the driveway leading to the stables.

Gramma Lisa drove past Allison's truck. "We'll want to allow the horses plenty of space to unload," she explained unnecessarily.

Sofia held back an eye roll as her grandmother found a parking spot in the lot beside the huge barn. With great difficulty, she waited for Gramma Lisa to shut off the engine, then counted to three before launching herself from the truck. She jogged in place, willing herself to wait for Gramma Lisa rather than bolt toward the horse trailer to check on Sundance.

"What a lovely day it's turned out to be," Gramma Lisa said when she finally got out of the truck.

Sofia nodded. "We'd better unload the horses before they get upset."

"I've got to find a bathroom first. Maybe you should, too."

This time, Sofia really did roll her eyes. "I'm going to check on Sundance."

Gramma Lisa laughed. "I'll see you in a few minutes."

Sofia hurried toward the trailer, arriving before Allison and Jess climbed out of the truck. Why were the adults being so slow? They had horses to unload. And to ride!

Without waiting for permission, Sofia opened the side door at the front of the trailer and stepped up into what Allison had called "the dressing room". The area, separated from the horses by a metal wall, was where they'd stored their tack and equipment needed for the weekend. She found Sundance's lead rope and slid his saddle from the rack above Magic's much heavier Western saddle. Had Gramma Lisa ever ridden Western? She supposed it wasn't that different from English, other than the horn in the front.

With her riding helmet and Sundance's lead rope and tack in hand, she hopped down from the dressing room and nearly collided with Allison. "Sorry," she gasped.

Allison pushed past her without a word.

"She's worried about Thor," Jess whispered in Sofia's ear while she gently guided her away from the door. "He gets a bit wound up...kind of like she does."

Allison emerged a moment later with a lead rope and a tense expression etched into her face. "Where's Lisa? We need to unload the horses. Now."

Sofia sucked in her lower lip. "She's looking for a bathroom."

"It's going to be okay, Allison," Jess said. "We need to get Sundance and Rosie off the trailer first. If she isn't back by then, I can handle Magic, too. Thor's going to be fine."

Allison frowned. "It's been a very long trailer ride for him, and you know how worked up he can get." She turned to Sofia. "Thor used to be a racehorse. Sometimes he thinks he still is."

Unsure of how else to respond, Sofia attempted a sympathetic nod while nervous thoughts bubbled through her mind. Sundance had competed with Magic. What if her horse tried to race against Thor, too? Would keeping him close to Rosie's side prevent him from bolting to the lead?

Allison didn't allow her time for further worry. "Are you ready?" She unlatched the trailer door without waiting for Sofia's answer.

Sundance turned his head sideways to stare at the unfamiliar surroundings. His ears pricked forward and he let out a rumbly whinny. Thor answered with an ear-splitting neigh, which was accompanied by a loud bang as his hoof smacked against the side of the trailer.

Sofia hurried into the trailer and laid her hand against Sundance's neck. "Don't worry. We're just going for a fun ride." She attached his lead rope to his halter and unclipped the trailer tie. "Ready?"

Sundance pushed his nose against her arm and gave it a shove. "I guess you are." She took a deep breath, hoping *she* was ready, too, and stepped down from the trailer. Sundance hopped out, his eyes wide and ears darting in all directions. Then he spun in a tight circle, as if he wanted to get back into the trailer with Rosie.

"Your girlfriend is coming," Jess said as she grinned at Sofia. She released the metal barrier that had separated Rosie from Sundance, swinging it forward until it rested against the wall where Sundance had been tied.

Sundance nickered at Rosie, who followed Jess out of the trailer. Thor whinnied again, even louder than before.

"Cut that out!" Allison bellowed at her horse.

Jess held out her hand, offering Rosie's lead rope to Allison. "Can you hold her for a second while I unload Magic? Then you can get Thor."

Allison nodded. "Please move your horse so he's not in the way," she said to Sofia as she led Rosie away from the trailer. She hadn't yelled. She hadn't even raised her voice, but Sofia flushed with a mixture of embarrassment and annoyance.

Gramma Lisa strode up to Sofia and Sundance. "So, you got started without me."

"Thor's acting up. Allison wants us to hurry," Sofia muttered, irritated with Allison's bossiness. The woman was worse than Olivia. Well, maybe not *worse*, but at least Sofia knew Olivia was her friend. Allison acted like Sofia was an ignorant little kid who didn't belong with the grownup riders.

Jess led Magic from the trailer and handed his lead to Gramma Lisa. "I hope you didn't have to pee behind a bush," she said, laughing.

Gramma Lisa chuckled. "If I did, would I admit it in front of my granddaughter?" She ran her fingers through Magic's thick, black mane. "He's such a handsome horse. Is he a Percheron?"

"His mom was a Percheron. His dad? Well, that's a story—"

"Will you *please* move your horse?" Allison interrupted.

Thor screeched for a third time. Allison said a rude word and shoved Rosie's lead rope into Jess's hands.

More banging noises and swearing followed. A minute or two later, Thor leaped from the trailer, followed by Allison, who desperately gripped the end of his lead rope as he dragged her forward.

"Alrighty then," Jess said, rolling her eyes.

Sofia immediately understood why Jason had described Thor as a monster Thoroughbred. The dark bay gelding towered over Rosie and Sundance, matching Magic's height, with a lighter, but muscular build. Since Allison owned Thor while she and Jess were still in college, he must have retired from racing years earlier, but he looked as if he'd give the Kentucky Derby winner a run for his money.

"I need to walk him around before I saddle him," Allison called out as Thor jigged past them.

Jess rubbed her temples. "I'm sorry," she muttered. "I'd forgotten about...well, never mind. Let's tie our horses to the trailer and get them groomed and tacked up before Thor comes back."

"Good plan," Gramma Lisa said.

Sofia glanced at petite Allison as she struggled to keep her high-spirited *monster* from ripping her arms from their sockets. She almost felt sorry for the woman.

She tied Sundance to the side of the trailer next to Rosie. His ears darted back and forth, taking in the unfamiliar sounds. His nostrils quivered. "You'll be fine," she said, willing herself to believe her own promise. Sundance would be with Rosie and Magic, who'd been to Acadia several times in the past. They would keep him calm and safe. Thor? She'd just keep her distance and hope for the best.

Jess ran a brush over Rosie's back and under her belly, ignoring Allison's intermittent swear words and Thor's high-pitched whinnies. "I suggest you stick close to me when we ride," she said in a low voice.

Sofia nodded.

It only took a few minutes to tack the horses. Gramma Lisa asked Jess to check that she'd fastened Magic's cinch properly. "I've only ridden in a Western saddle once before," she admitted.

Sofia double checked the tightness of Sundance's English girth while they were busy inspecting Magic's tack. It wouldn't do to have her saddle slip while they were half-way up the mountain.

Allison and Thor returned to the trailer just as Sofia was buckling Sundance's noseband. The dark bay Thoroughbred snorted, though he looked a bit less anxious than he had a few minutes before.

"Do you think you could hold him for me while I tack him up?" Allison asked Jess. "He might pull back if I tie him to the trailer."

Jess sighed before taking his lead rope.

Gramma Lisa led Magic in a wide arc around Thor as she made her way around the trailer to Sofia's side. "Are you all set? Do you want me to check your—"

"I'm all set," Sofia said, trying not to snap. "His girth is tight," she said in a softer tone. "And I've buckled my helmet."

"Then you're ready to mount up." Gramma Lisa glanced at Thor. "Might be a good idea to do it now. I suspect once he's tacked, Allison won't want to wait around. Can I at least hold Sundance for you?"

"Sure." It wasn't worth arguing about it. Sofia slid down his stirrup leathers and stuck her toe into the left stirrup. She hopped from the ground and swung her leg over Sundance's back, settling into his saddle in one fluid motion. Gramma Lisa should be impressed with her mounting skills.

Gramma Lisa had a more difficult time climbing into Magic's saddle. Of course, he was six inches taller than Sundance and Gramma Lisa was considerably older than Sofia, but Sofia couldn't suppress a tiny grin.

They only had to wait for another minute or two before Allison, with Jess's help, was astride Thor. The Thoroughbred danced under her. "I'm going to ride him up the road a few hundred yards to settle him down while the rest of you get ready," she announced, as if she'd been waiting for them rather than the other way around.

Jess stepped sideways to avoid being run over by Thor as he trotted away. "This should be interesting," she said under her breath.

Sofia hoped it wouldn't be *too* interesting.

Chapter 24

Sofia circled Sundance around Magic and Gramma Lisa, struggling to contain his energy as Thor trotted up the road away from the group. She tugged on his reins while he pranced excitedly under her, his hindquarters bunching, ready to catapult them forward and race after Allison's Thoroughbred. Sofia didn't know how fast her palomino could run, but there was a reason his breed was called the Quarter Horse. They could explode from a halt to a full out gallop and cover a quarter of a mile in twenty-one seconds. Thoroughbreds might be famous for being racehorses, but Quarter Horses were the fastest sprinting horses in the world. They could reach top speeds of fifty-five miles per hour, which would leave even a Triple Crown-winning Thoroughbred in the dust.

Did Sundance possess *that* kind of speed? The thought both thrilled and terrified Sofia.

Gramma Lisa frowned. "Are you sure you're—"

"I'm fine," Sofia hissed. What was she going to do now, anyway? Dismount and wait at the trailer with Sundance while the rest of them rode for two hours? She'd just have to stay next to Rosie and hope his affection for the Appaloosa would keep his competitive spirit in check.

Jess mounted Rosie. "Are we ready to ride up Day Mountain?"

Sofia sucked in a breath and nodded.

Gramma Lisa gave a quick glance at Sofia. "We're just going to be walking, right?"

"Sure," Jess said. "Magic is a really good boy, but of course you'll want a bit of time getting to know him. We don't have to trot or canter until you feel ready."

"Uh…" Gramma Lisa said. "I'm sure he's going to be fine. I just…"

Sofia held back a snicker.

"So, are we ready?" Jess asked.

Gramma Lisa glanced at Sofia again before answering. "Yes, but let's keep it nice and slow."

"Sure thing." Jess brushed her legs against Rosie's sides, and the mare stepped forward eagerly.

Sundance followed behind them without waiting for Sofia's permission. She should correct him, but if she forced him to wait, he'd probably toss his head and prance. Better to let him get away with a minor act of disobedience than to risk him bolting after Thor, who was now trotting back toward their group. Gramma Lisa and Magic fell into place behind Sundance.

With Thor jigging in the lead, they passed Wildwood's main barn and headed gradually uphill. The carriage road was unpaved, but its surface was smooth and firm. They crossed over a wide stone bridge and turned to the right.

The road looked like it had been carefully carved into the landscape around the mountain. A steep, rocky hill rose up to their left. Trees lined both sides of the trail, their branches mostly stripped bare of leaves, allowing Sofia to peer into the woods above and below.

Large, grayish-white granite coping stones guarded the right side of the road. Each block had slightly different shapes, some rectangular, some rounded, and a few with jagged, pointed edges. Most were around two feet high and three feet wide, spaced about a foot apart. As they continued along the road, Sofia marveled at just how many there were. Hundreds? Thousands? Was every carriage trail outlined in this way?

"They're called Rockefeller's Teeth," Jess explained. "The land here used to be owned by a very rich family named the Rockefellers. John D. Rockefeller Jr. loved horses. He started building these carriage trails in 1913. Cars had taken over the roads by then, and he wanted to create a beautiful place where people could ride and drive their horses without the danger of cars. It took twenty-seven years to finish the project, but when it was done, he'd constructed fifty-one miles of roads. He donated it all to make this park."

"A very generous gift," Gramma Lisa said. She appeared much more at ease now that they'd ridden for ten minutes without Sundance bolting after Thor, who had finally relaxed into a normal, brisk walk.

Sofia realized she'd relaxed, too. She closed her eyes, feeling Sundance's body gently sway from side to side with each stride and listening to the horses' hooves as they clopped against the road. She breathed in the scent of damp leaves mixed with just a hint of a salty sea breeze.

Sundance blew a long, fluttery breath from his nostrils, a sign he was enjoying their ride as much as Sofia. "You're a good boy," she said, taking the reins into one hand and leaning forward to run her fingers along his neck.

Allison twisted sideways in the saddle and turned her head to look over her shoulder. "Is anyone up for a trot?"

Sofia grinned. "Yes!"

Jess glanced behind her at Gramma Lisa.

"As long as it's just a trot," Gramma Lisa said. "A nice, in control trot."

"Of course," Allison said. Was it Sofia's imagination, or did the woman sound a bit insulted, as if Thor were the calmest, most obedient horse in the world, and Gramma Lisa had dared to imply otherwise?

Sofia repositioned her hands on the reins and sat straighter in the saddle. She glanced at Jess, who smiled and nodded. She squeezed Sundance's sides, urging him to break into a trot alongside Rosie. The two horses surged forward at the same moment, their hooves ringing in tandem against the hard surface of the road.

Ahead, Thor tossed his head and swished his long, black tail, obviously annoyed Allison hadn't allowed him to canter, but he settled down after a few hundred yards.

As the horses trotted up the gradual slope of the road, the trees thinned out, revealing a vista that nearly took Sofia's breath away. She hadn't realized they'd already climbed so high. The ground beyond the granite coping stones fell away below them, stretching through miles of forest, the dark green shapes of spruce and fir mixed with shades of rusty oak leaves and patches of golden beech. And beyond that, the sparkling ocean, set against a bright blue sky.

She'd never trotted for this long before. Despite the cool temperature, beads of sweat dampened her forehead and dribbled down her back. She wished she could strip off her coat. Was Sundance getting tired? She leaned forward in the saddle to touch her horse's shoulder, but didn't dare to bend down far enough to feel his chest.

Sofia studied Rosie's frosted chestnut coat. It looked damp. Trotting up a mountain, even a small one, must be a lot of work. Shouldn't they give their horses a rest?

Jess caught Sofia's gaze and smiled. "Having fun?"

"Yeah, but I'm kind of wondering..." she hesitated, not wanting to sound like a wimp. "How long do you think we're going to be trotting? I mean, I'm doing fine, but I don't want to make the horses too tired."

Jess nodded. "I'd forgotten how much of a speed demon Allison is. She'd probably gallop the whole way up if we weren't here. But look, even Thor is getting lathered between his hind legs."

"I wouldn't complain if we took a breather," Gramma Lisa called out from behind them.

"Hey, Allison," Jess shouted to her friend, who was at least fifty feet in front of Sundance and Rosie. "Let's walk for a bit."

Allison didn't respond. The sharp ringing of hooves had probably drowned out Jess's voice. Jess shouted again, louder.

Thor and Allison continued to trot briskly up the carriage road.

"Let me see if I can catch up to her," Jess said. She urged Rosie into a canter.

Sundance surged forward to keep up with his friend. "No, Sundance!" Sofia pulled back on his reins. He raised his head and strained against the bit. The further ahead Rosie cantered, the more Sundance fought for control.

"Hold him back, Sofia!" Gramma Lisa yelled, as if Sofia wasn't trying as hard as she could to slow her horse, who was now cantering a stride or two behind Rosie.

Sofia leaned her weight back in the saddle and continued to tug on Sundance's reins. The palomino shook his head from side to side.

Jess looked back. "Oh!" She slowed her Appaloosa back into a trot. "I'm so sorry, Sofia."

Sundance slowed his pace to match Rosie's, falling in by her side as if nothing had happened. Sofia wished she could take credit for bringing him back under control, but she couldn't kid herself. Sundance had completely ignored her, preferring to follow the lead of his new best friend.

"Let's just walk for now," Jess said. "Allison will figure it out soon enough. If she doesn't, well, we'll meet her at the top."

"We should probably walk the rest of the way," Gramma Lisa said. "Magic is winded, and the horses are sweating."

Sofia sighed. Her grandmother had tried to make it sound like she was only concerned about the fitness level of their horses, but it was clear her real worry was about whether Sofia could handle her own horse. And as much as she wanted to deny it, Sofia had to admit she'd lost control over Sundance. Maybe she'd never even had it at all.

Chapter 25

Allison didn't notice their absence, or, at least, she hadn't slowed her pace or turned back to join them. Sofia was relieved not to have to deal with the uptight woman or her monster Thoroughbred. This was supposed to be a family trip, and it felt like Allison had crashed the party. Of course, they wouldn't be here at all if it hadn't been for Allison's invitation. And her horse trailer. And her cousin with the boarding stable in Bar Harbor. *Just a few minor details.*

Without the pressure of Allison and Thor's anxious presence, Sofia, Jess, Gramma Lisa, and their horses ambled along the side of Day Mountain, enjoying the spectacular views of Seal Harbor and the islands below. They rode in silence, except for the clopping of their horses' hooves.

Sofia waved to a man and two children who passed them on the other side of the carriage road as they made their way down.

The girl, a few years younger than Sofia, tugged on her father's coat. "Dad, look at the palomino! He's so pretty."

"Thanks," Sofia said. "His name is Sundance."

"You're so lucky," the girl said. "Can I pat him?"

Sofia glanced at Jess, who smiled and halted Rosie. Before Sofia asked him, Sundance stopped, too. She should have corrected her horse and made him wait for her signal, but the girl and her younger brother were already jogging over to meet them.

"Don't run," the father called out to his kids, who ignored his instructions much like Sundance had ignored Sofia's.

The little boy reached his hand toward Sundance's nose. "He's a nice horse. Not like the one back there." He pointed up the trail.

"That lady was mean," the girl said as she touched Sundance's sweaty neck. "She yelled at us when we wanted to pat her horse."

Were they talking about Allison?

"She just didn't want you to get hurt," the father said. "You must be careful around horses. They're a lot bigger than you."

"Was that horse a big, bay Thoroughbred?" Gramma Lisa asked.

"Uh..." The man stroked his stubbly chin. "It was big. And, uh, dark brownish color? It was going kind of fast, and the woman riding it didn't stop."

Jess laughed. "Sounds like Allison and Thor. How far ahead of us are they?"

The man shrugged. "She passed us about five or ten minutes ago."

Gramma Lisa sighed. "She's probably at the top by now."

Allison would have to wait for them. It served her right. She might get annoyed, but it wasn't like she would leave Acadia without the other horses, would she?

The girl tapped Sofia's leg. "Can I have a ride?"

"Me too!" The boy whined.

"No, you can't ride," their father said. "Give the pretty horse another pat and let them be on their way."

"I want to pat the black one, too," the boy said.

"Jared." The man reached for his son's hand. "It's time to go. Sophia, come along."

"That's my name, too," Sofia said to the girl. "I hope you get your own horse to ride someday."

The girl grinned. "He's going to be a palomino, just like yours."

"Thank you, Sofia," the father said. "I hope you and your family have a wonderful ride." He took his daughter's hand and led his children away from Sundance and the other horses.

Sofia turned her head, watching for a moment as the family continued down the carriage road. She swallowed, but it didn't push away the lump forming in her throat. Two years ago, her dream of owning a palomino horse seemed like an impossible fantasy, and yet, here she was, riding Sundance up a mountain. Two years ago, she barely remembered her grandmother, and yet, here she was with Gramma Lisa riding by her side. Two years ago, her father hadn't been a part of her life...and now? Was he?

She shifted in the saddle and gave Sundance's sides a squeeze. Daddy said he wanted to be a part of her life. They'd exchanged a few letters and talked on a video call. He'd even given her plane tickets to visit him in Florida over Christmas. Yet none of it felt real. When was the last time her father had held her hand, like Jared and Sophia's dad, or taken her on a hike? She couldn't remember.

Sofia had a father. And a stepmother. She had an abuela and aunts and uncles and cousins. And soon, she'd have a baby brother. But she didn't have a relationship with any of them. Would that change when she visited them next month? And what would happen when she returned to her everyday life in Maine? Would they go back to being strangers?

"The horses have had a nice rest. Do you feel up to another trot?" Jess asked. "Nothing fast or crazy."

"Sure." Sofia hoped Sundance understood the part about not being *fast* or *crazy*.

"I suppose," Gramma Lisa said. Sofia couldn't see her reaction, but at least she hadn't said no.

Sofia urged Sundance forward before Jess asked Rosie to trot. Sundance needed to listen to her instead of blindly following the Appaloosa's every move. He trotted ahead of Rosie for a few strides before the mare caught up.

"Onward and upwards," Jess said as the two horses trotted side by side to the top of Day Mountain.

Sofia lowered the visor on the passenger side of Gramma Lisa's truck, shielding her eyes from the setting sun's low rays so she could focus on the trailer in front of them. Gramma Lisa's visor was down, too, but the sunglasses she wore must have allowed her to see better than Sofia could.

They'd spoken little since loading the horses into the trailer while the scowling Allison had looked on. Jess's friend had muttered some less than kind words about how long she'd had to wait for them to arrive back at Wildwood Stables after their ride. Jess had muttered a few words back about not realizing it had been a race to the top of the mountain.

Sofia's phone vibrated with a text from Daddy. Had he remembered her trip to Acadia? Was he texting to ask how the ride had gone? She stared at the message.

Daniella has gone into the hospital. Her blood pressure is too high, so the doctors want to monitor her overnight. Don't worry. Your brother is fine, but please pray that he waits for a few more weeks before he's born.

Sofia emitted a squeaky gasp and placed the phone on her lap.

Gramma Lisa glanced at her. "What's wrong?"

"It's from my father." Sofia sucked in her lower lip.

"Oh? What did he want?" Why was Gramma Lisa still looking at her? She should keep her focus on driving.

Sofia tugged on the end of her frizzy ponytail. "His wife is in the hospital. Her blood pressure is too high."

"Preeclampsia?" Gramma Lisa said, returning her attention to the road.

"He didn't tell me what it's called." Sofia tried to push away her growing unease. If Daddy said not to worry, surely Daniella and Santiago weren't in danger.

"Do you know when the baby is due?"

"In five weeks." What if Santiago was born too early?

"Well, I hope she can hang on for another few weeks, then," Gramma Lisa said.

"Daddy wants me to pray."

Gramma Lisa nodded. "That's a good thing to do, but don't get too worried. She's in the hospital, and the doctors and nurses will keep them safe. Even if your brother is born early, he's going to be fine."

How could Gramma Lisa know that for certain?

Sofia closed her eyes. *God, please keep Daniella and my brother safe.*

Chapter 26

It was nearly dark by the time they arrived at Sullivan Family Stables outside of Ellsworth. The two large pastures on either side of the driveway appeared to be empty, but a tiny gray pony, not much bigger than Snickers, paced along the fence line in a small paddock beside the barn. His high-pitched neighing was met with Thor's anxious whinnies, followed by Sundance's lower rumbling call.

Stomach churning, Sofia hurried out of the truck. The last thing she needed was for Allison to yell at her for taking too long to unload Sundance. She'd texted Daddy a few minutes earlier, asking whether Daniella had what Gramma Lisa called *preeclampsia*, but he hadn't answered. Did that mean something even worse had happened to her stepmother? Was Santiago about to be born prematurely?

She paced behind the horse trailer, unsure of whether she should get the lead rope from the storage area in the front or wait for Jess and Allison. For a woman who'd been in such a rush all day, Allison was taking a ridiculously long time to get out of her truck.

Gramma Lisa joined Sofia. "This looks like a nice place."

Sofia nodded, though she hadn't noticed much about the property. She forced herself to look around.

The stable was much bigger than Stephanie's or Gramma Lisa's, though not as large as the historic barn at Wildwood. The gray pony peered out at them from between wooden fence boards, painted white. A three-sided shelter stood at the back of the paddock. Sofia squinted. It was difficult to make out in the growing darkness, but was there another pony, too? No, a donkey! She smiled despite herself, thinking of Tootsie and her chubby goat companions.

She turned to the sound of another vehicle making its way up the driveway. Allison climbed out of her truck, followed by Jess.

"It's about time," Allison muttered as the approaching vehicle passed them.

The driver parked in front of the barn. A little boy hopped out from the back seat and raced toward them. "I'm here to help!"

"Slow down, Caden," an older boy called after him. He looked to be around Sofia's age, with thick, curly hair, almost as dark as Sofia's.

The driver closed her door with a loud *thump*. "I'm sorry, Allison. We didn't expect you for another half hour," she said. "Caden! Don't you dare get in that trailer! Logan, could you please take your brother into the barn?"

Caden crossed his arms over his tiny chest. "I want to help!"

"You can help by making sure our guests' horses have full water buckets."

Logan grabbed his brother's arm. "Come on. We can check on Hawk and Cowboy."

Caden stomped his foot, but reluctantly followed Logan into the barn.

"Welcome to Sullivan Family Stables." The short plump woman, who must have been Caden and Logan's mother, smiled at Gramma Lisa and Sofia. "I'm Allison's cousin, Nicole. Did you have a nice ride this afternoon? It turned out to be a lovely day."

"Wonderful, thank you," Gramma Lisa said.

Wonderful? Sofia glanced at her grandmother. Despite their rocky start, it had been wonderful, she realized, after Allison and Thor had taken off on their own.

"Thank you so much for letting us board the horses for the weekend," Jess said. "And for allowing me and Allison to bunk at your house. It's very generous of you."

Nicole waved her hand. "It's nothing. As you can see, we've got plenty of room. It's just our animals and one boarder for now. But we have big plans for—"

"Can we *please* unload the horses?" Allison interrupted.

Sofia rolled her eyes. Jason once had a crush on this rude woman? Mom had *nothing* to worry about, that was for sure.

"Of course." Nicole's mouth formed a hard line.

Jess glared at Allison. "We'd love to hear about your plans for the place after we get the horses settled in. Wouldn't we, Allison?"

Allison didn't bother to respond. She just stood there, glaring back at Jess. Had they gotten into a disagreement while driving from Acadia to Sullivan Family Stables?

Gramma Lisa nudged Sofia's arm. "Why don't you get Sundance's lead rope so you can unload him?"

Sofia walked to the front of the trailer, thankful Allison and Jess wouldn't be staying at the motel with them. Mom, Grampy, and Jason were already there, waiting for their arrival. Unfortunately, Jason had invited *all* of them to dinner at a restaurant he and Jess had visited on previous trips to Acadia. Maybe Allison would decide not to join them.

Lead rope now in hand, Sofia hurried back before Allison complained about something else.

Sundance's nostrils quivered. "You're going to stay here with Rosie," Sofia assured him while she clipped the lead rope to his halter. "Don't worry. It's just for the weekend. I'll be back tomorrow."

He waited for Sofia to step down before hopping out of the trailer to join her.

"Good boy, Sundance." Sofia led him away from the trailer and scratched his neck. He leaned against her hand. "You like that, don't you?"

Sundance nickered when Rosie stepped out of the trailer.

Jess grinned at Sofia. "Let's get these two lovebirds into the barn."

"Logan will show you around," Nicole said. "I'm sure Caden will, too. You have my permission to yell at him if he gets in the way, though."

Sofia blinked as her eyes adjusted to the bright light inside the stable. Like most of the barns she'd visited, there was a central aisle with rows of box stalls on either side, but unlike other barns she'd seen, these stalls didn't have doors. Nylon mesh barriers, about a foot and a half wide, stretched over the openings to prevent horses from wandering into the barn aisle. Couldn't a horse climb over it or crawl under it or simply muscle right through the stall guard? Would Sundance?

A reddish-chestnut horse with a wide star between his brown eyes leaned over his stall guard and whinnied. Across the aisle, a buckskin flattened his ears and shook his head at Rosie.

Logan pointed at the buckskin. "Don't be a grump, Cowboy."

Caden danced in front of the chestnut horse. "Hawk wants to meet your horses!"

"Calm down, or you'll spook their horses," Logan chided. "The Appaloosa can go in the stall next to Hawk. And you can put the palomino next to Cowboy."

Sofia hesitated. What if Cowboy broke through his stall and attacked Sundance during the night? "Uh, if it's okay, can Sundance go into the stall next to Rosie? They're good friends."

Logan shrugged. "Doesn't matter to me. We have four stalls ready, so the other two horses can go next to Cowboy."

Relieved, Sofia led Sundance into the stall beside Rosie. He sniffed the empty feed trough, then the water bucket, before pawing at the thick bedding of wood shavings. "We'll bring you your grain and hay in a few minutes," Sofia told him.

Heavy hooves clopped against the concrete barn aisle. "Where do you want me to put Magic?" Gramma Lisa asked.

"He can go next to this one." Logan waved his arms at Cowboy to force his menacing face away from the barn aisle while Magic passed the buckskin's stall.

Magic didn't appear to care about his new neighbor's aggressive antics. He followed Gramma Lisa into the stall, and, like Sundance had, explored the feed trough. Finding nothing, he grunted, bent his knees, and eased himself to the floor. Gramma Lisa laughed as the half-Percheron rolled in the clean bedding, coating his entire body in wood shavings. He stood and shook like a dog.

Caden giggled. "He's silly. Can I brush him?"

Logan shook his head. "You know you're not allowed to touch the clients' horses."

The little boy pouted. "Mom lets me brush Cowboy sometimes."

"You can pet my horse," Sofia offered. How long would she have to wait before her little brother was old enough to brush Sundance? "How old are you?"

Caden puffed out his chest. "Five and a half. I have my own pony. Her name is Princess, and I won a blue ribbon with her."

"Everyone got a blue ribbon," Logan said. "It's not like you had to do anything except for sit in the saddle while Mom led you around."

Jess laughed. "I'm sure you and Princess were amazing. Is she the gray pony in the paddock outside?"

Caden stuck his tongue out at his brother. "Yeah. She lives with Freddy. He's a miniature donkey."

"I've got a mini donkey, too," Jess said. "Her name is Tootsie."

"Woah. Woah!" Allison shouted as Thor dragged her through the barn door.

Nicole followed close behind. "Caden, get out of the way!"

Caden stood in the middle of the aisle, staring open-mouthed at the enormous Thoroughbred. Logan grabbed his brother's arm and yanked him sideways.

Cowboy strained against his stall guard, his ears flattened and his teeth barred.

Thor snorted. Then he lunged at Cowboy!

"No!" Allison screamed, a moment too late.

Thor reared.

Cowboy flew backward, avoiding Thor's slashing hooves, but as Thor attempted to pull away, his front right leg caught against the stall guard. Sofia stared in horror as Allison's panicked horse thrashed wildly to free himself from the barrier, which held fast. Thor's hind legs scrambled sideways along the concrete floor.

"Get out of his way! He's going to fall!" Nicole shouted at Allison.

Allison released her grip on Thor's lead rope and jumped away a split second before the metal hooks holding the stall guard tore free from the wall. The Thoroughbred crashed to the floor.

"Don't let that nasty beast attack Thor!" Allison cried.

Cowboy cowered in the back of his stall, clearly shaken by what had just occurred. He'd made a nasty face, but he hadn't been the one to attack Thor. It had been the other way around.

Thor scrambled to his feet.

"Is he hurt?" Gramma Lisa asked from inside Magic's stall. If she'd been in the barn aisle instead... No, Sofia didn't want to think about what might have happened.

Nicole hurried to Allison's side. "Let's get him away from Cowboy and check him over. Logan? Can you please halter Cowboy and stay with him until we can repair the stall guard?"

"Why don't you have proper doors?" Allison demanded. "Your setup is dangerous."

"Your *horse* is dangerous," Logan shot back.

"Logan, please stay out of this," Nicole said. "We need to make sure Thor hasn't been hurt." She ran her hands along his front legs, ignoring Allison's huffing noises.

After Nicole determined that Thor's only injury was a small scrape where his right forearm had rubbed against the nylon, she turned her attention to repairing Cowboy's stall guard.

Sofia glanced at her phone. There was still no response from her father, but Mom had texted to ask when they'd finish putting the horses away. Though she didn't want to leave Sundance, the sooner she got away from Allison, the better. "I'll get their hay from the trailer."

"I can help," Caden said.

"Don't be stupid," Logan said from inside Cowboy's stall. "You're not strong enough. Why don't you hold Cowboy for me while I help?"

Caden scowled. "I'm not stupid."

Nicole sighed. "Logan, don't call your brother stupid."

Sofia would never treat her little brother that way. Of course, they'd be living two thousand miles apart, so she might not have many opportunities to interact with him. Not like Logan and Caden. Or Olivia and Ryan. "Caden can help me. I'm sure he's very strong."

The little boy grinned. "See, Logan? She *wants* me to help."

Sofia patted Sundance and ducked under the stall guard. "I'm going to be a big sister soon," she whispered to Caden. *Hopefully not too soon, though.*

Chapter 27

Daddy's text arrived as Gramma Lisa pulled into the parking lot of the Sunrise Motel. Sofia closed her eyes and sucked in a breath before reading it.

Yes, it's called preeclampsia, but please don't worry. The doctors and nurses are taking good care of Daniella.

Sofia read the message a second time. That was it? Nothing about Santiago? Was Daddy deliberately hiding information from her, or did he have nothing more to report?

Gramma Lisa switched off the truck's engine. "Was it from your father?"

Sofia nodded. "Daniella has preeclampsia, but he says not to worry because the doctors and nurses are taking care of her."

"I know it sounds scary, but I'm sure your father is right. Besides, worrying won't change anything."

Sofia unfastened her seatbelt. *Easy for you to say. Your brother isn't in danger.* But what Gramma Lisa said was true. There was nothing she could do to help Daniella or Santiago.

Except...

She could pray again. Would God listen? Maybe she should text Olivia and ask her to tell Pastor Amy about the situation. God might respond better to a professional.

Gramma Lisa opened her door. "Are you coming?"

"Give me a minute. I have to..." Sofia hesitated. Gramma Lisa wasn't religious. She probably wouldn't understand. "Uh...text Olivia."

"I can wait for you."

Sofia shook her head. "I can meet you in the lobby."

Gramma Lisa shrugged. "If that's what you want."

Sofia waited until her grandmother walked all the way across the parking lot and in through the large glass doors before she folded her hands on her lap and closed her eyes. "God," she whispered. "Please keep Daniella and my brother safe. I'm really scared he's going to be born too early." She sighed. "And, if it's not too much to ask, can you please make Allison a little nicer? And her horse, too? And keep us safe when we ride tomorrow? Thanks. Amen."

Just to be safe, she texted Olivia, too. *Daniella is in the hospital. Can you ask your mom to pray for her and my baby brother?* Sofia was about to hit send when she realized Olivia would get annoyed if she didn't also tell her about their trip. She added two more brief sentences.

We rode up Day Mountain. Everything is going great. She'd report the *true* story later.

Sofia shoved her phone into her backpack, opened the truck door, and headed for the motel lobby.

Sofia twisted the motel room's shower faucet to the left, attempting to cool the sweltering water to a more tolerable temperature. She yelped as her steamy shower suddenly transformed into an icy waterfall only a penguin would love. Fiddling with the faucet brought the temperature up a few degrees to a barely acceptable lukewarm, but she feared scalding herself if she turned the knob further.

Mom rapped on the bathroom door. At least she *hoped* it was Mom. Sofia wanted to sleep in Gramma Lisa's motel room, but Mom had acted hurt when Sofia suggested it. "Honey Bear," Mom had said. "You'll be with your grandmother all day. I want to spend some time with you during our family trip."

"You need to hurry," Mom called from just inside the bathroom door. "We're leaving for dinner in ten minutes."

"You're the one who told me I had to take a shower," Sofia grumbled.

"Ten minutes." Mom closed the door.

Sofia rinsed the lather from her body and contemplated whether she could get away without shampooing her hair. Mom washed her straight blonde locks every day and seemed incapable of understanding that Sofia's thick curly hair required much less frequent washing than her own. "I'll just tell her there wasn't time," Sofia said out loud as she turned off the water.

She wrapped herself in the thin, scratchy motel towel and checked her phone. Olivia had responded with a prayer hands emoji and a request for more details about their ride.

"Honey Bear," Mom called out. "Five minutes!"

Sofia shook her head and returned her phone to the edge of the sink.

It didn't look like Gramma Lisa had washed her frizzy gray hair, either. She'd changed from her smelly horse clothes into rumpled tan slacks and a dark blue sweater. Mom, of course, had dressed like a fashion model in the short red dress and heels she'd worn on her first date with Jason. Olivia would certainly approve.

To Sofia's surprise, Mom hadn't forced her to wear the dress she'd packed for her. Instead, she'd allowed her to wear a clean sweatshirt and jeans if she promised to wear the dress during their next dinner out. Mom must have been desperate to get Sofia out of their room and into the motel lobby to meet Grampy and Jason on time.

When they arrived at the lobby, Grampy was seated in a puffy fake-leather armchair across from a gas-powered fireplace. Beside him sat a much younger redheaded man wearing a light blue shirt and navy tie. When Grampy stood to greet them, the other man stood, too, and grinned at them.

Sofia's mouth fell open in astonishment. The tall, clean-shaven man was Jason!

Jason's grin widened, and he winked at Sofia. "Surprise!"

Mom appeared just as stunned as Sofia. "You shaved it off!"

Jason ran his fingers over his clean-shaven chin. "I figured it was time to stop looking like a hick from the sticks. I hope you like it." He kissed Mom on the cheek.

"I don't know how you looked before," Gramma Lisa said, "but your new look suits you. I'm Mandi's mother, Lisa Richardson."

Jason held out his hand. "It's such a pleasure to meet you, finally, Ms. Richardson."

Gramma Lisa chuckled and took his hand. "Lisa is fine."

"Yes, Ma'am. I hope you and Sofia had an excellent ride this afternoon."

"We did, thank you," Gramma Lisa said.

Sofia rolled her eyes. Everyone was acting like their ride had been perfect, but she was tired of pretending. "You were right, Jason. Thor is a monster Thoroughbred—an evil monster. And don't even get me started on Allison."

Gramma Lisa guffawed. Apparently, she was sick of pretending, too.

Jason's eyebrows shot up at the sound of Gramma Lisa's raucous laughter, a noise remarkably similar to Tootsie's bray.

Mom's face flushed pink. "Tone it down, Mum."

Gramma Lisa covered her mouth.

"Mom, you have nothing to worry about with Allison," Sofia continued. Now that she'd finally released her feelings, it was impossible to rein them in. "She's a rude, uptight, control freak. I can't believe we have to eat dinner with her."

"Sofia." Gramma Lisa shook her head, unsuccessfully hiding her smirk. "Don't forget that our ride wouldn't have happened without Allison and her cousin's hospitality."

Jason stroked the place where his scraggly beard used to be. "She used to be a bit of a high maintenance person. Jess thought she'd outgrown that."

"She hasn't," Sofia said.

"Now that you've aired your true feelings about the young woman," Grampy said, "let's try to keep the Allison bashing to a minimum while we meet her and Jess for dinner."

"Sorry." Sofia sucked in her lower lip, stung by Grampy's disapproving tone. Maybe it *had* been unfair to criticize Allison in front of everyone, but he hadn't just spent the day with her. He'd discover the truth for himself soon enough.

But when Jess and Allison arrived at the restaurant a few minutes after Sofia and the others had been seated, things did not go as she'd expected.

"Sorry we're a bit late," Allison said sweetly. She wore a form-fitting black dress, even shorter than Mom's. Her hair and makeup were perfect, as if she'd spent the past few hours getting ready for a party instead of wrestling with her misbehaving horse. Though Sofia thought Jess was a much prettier woman than her uptight friend, she couldn't help noticing the way some of the men in the restaurant watched Allison as she walked toward their table. Even Grampy smiled at her a bit too long, in Sofia's opinion.

Like Sofia and Gramma Lisa, Jess looked like she'd taken the minimum effort necessary to clean up after their full day with the horses. She'd changed into a creamy white sweater and a slightly rumpled, flowy green skirt, but a strand of hay poked out from her messy ponytail. She pointed at her chin and stared at Jason. "Who kidnapped my brother?"

Jason rose from the table, grinning.

"Nice to see you again, Jason." Allison sauntered over to him, threw her arms around his shoulders, and kissed him on the cheek.

He quickly slipped from her embrace. "Uh, Allison?" Jason's face flushed. "I'd like to introduce you to my girlfriend, Mandi, and her family."

Allison lifted her chin and smiled at Mom. "So nice to meet you, Mandi."

Mom glared back.

So did Sofia.

"And, uh, you've met her daughter, Sofia, of course," Jason stammered. "And Mandi's mother, Ms. Richardson."

"Just Lisa is fine," Gramma Lisa said, shaking her head slightly at Jason.

"And Mr. Richardson. He's Mandi's grandfather and Sofia's great-grandfather."

"That makes me sound so old." Grampy pushed back his chair and stood. "You can call me Bill."

Allison flashed a dazzling smile at him. "Nice to meet you, Bill."

Sofia balled her fists under the table. Didn't Grampy realize what Allison was doing? It wasn't enough for this horrible woman and her horrible horse to ruin their riding trip. Now she wanted to steal Jason away from Mom...and from her!

It wouldn't work.

It couldn't work.

Jess pulled out the empty chair next to Grampy and sat. Grampy blinked, apparently realizing that Allison was not going to give *him* a hug, and returned to his seat. Thankfully, the only remaining chair was at the opposite end of the table from Jason, next to Gramma Lisa.

"What a lovely restaurant." Allison sat, ignoring Mom's continued glare. "What are you all ordering?"

"I'm getting a lobster," Jess said.

"That's pretty messy." Allison glanced down at her dress. "Do you suppose you can order it already out of the shell?"

"Lazy man's lobster," Gramma Lisa said, pointing to her menu. Was it Sofia's imagination, or had Gramma Lisa drawn out the word *lazy* a bit too long, like she might be implying something negative about Allison's preferences?

"I'd like lobster, too," Sofia said. "The *regular* kind."

"Me, too," Jason said. "Shell and all. Puts hair on your chest."

Sofia's face contorted with the effort of suppressing a snicker.

Allison's nose wrinkled. "It does what?"

Grampy's mustache twitched.

Jess covered her mouth.

"Puts hair on your chest." Jason winked at Sofia, who could no longer hold back a howl of laughter.

Mom's lips puckered. Her shoulders began to shake. "I think I'll have a *regular* lobster, too," she said, giggling.

Gramma Lisa cocked her head at Mom and chuckled. "I suppose I'd better order one, too."

Jess grinned at the bewildered-looking Allison. "What can I say? My family is weird."

Sofia reached for Mom's hand and gave it a squeeze. "We are."

Chapter 28

"Good morning, Honey Bear," Mom said.

When Sofia groaned and pulled the bed sheet over her head, Mom gave her shoulder a gentle nudge.

"Come on. Rise and shine."

Was she late for school? Had she missed Sundance's feeding time? Sofia flung the sheet away from her face and flipped onto her back. Disoriented, she blinked at Mom and the unfamiliar pale-yellow wall behind her. The motel room!

Heart racing, Sofia leaped from the bed. Thick curtains covered the windows, making it impossible to tell whether the sun had risen yet. What if they'd taken the horses to Acadia without her? "What time is it?"

Mom smiled. "Eight-thirty. I don't think you've slept that late for months."

"The horses! They need to be fed!"

"Don't worry about that. Jess has it under control. She'll meet you and Gramma Lisa at that horse stable place in Acadia at ten."

"But I should help," Sofia protested.

Mom shook her head. "You were exhausted. Gramma Lisa told me you'd been up for hours before dawn yesterday. She also told me your stepmother is in the hospital. Why didn't you say any-thing to me?"

Because you always overreact or get jealous? Sofia wasn't about to tell her mother *that*. Instead, she sighed and walked over to the desk where she'd left her phone to charge overnight.

"Any updates from your father?" Mom asked.

"No."

Mom wrapped her arms around Sofia's slumped shoulders and kissed the top of her head. "You don't need to lock your feelings up inside you."

But I do. Mom hated Daddy. She'd made it perfectly clear that she didn't want him to be a part of Sofia's life. "Gramma Lisa says I shouldn't worry."

"That's always much easier said than done, isn't it?" Mom tightened her embrace. "It's okay to be worried sometimes."

Sofia's shoulders relaxed a bit, surprised by her mother's genuine support. She took a deep breath. "What if something bad happens to the baby? Like he's born too early? What if my brother isn't strong enough to...to make it?"

"Oh, Honey Bear, if your brother is born five weeks early, he might need some extra care in the hospital, but he's not going to die."

"Are you sure?"

Mom hesitated before answering. "We can never be one hundred percent sure about anything that will happen, but whatever happens, you don't need to face it alone."

Sofia buried her face in Mom's fluffy pajama top. The weight pressing against her chest lightened. Mom was right. She didn't have to face it alone. She had Mom and Grampy and Gramma Lisa...and Jason.

Mom stroked Sofia's hair. "Your brother is going to be so lucky to have a sister like you."

Sofia and Gramma Lisa pulled into the Wildwood Stables parking lot before Jess and Allison arrived with the horses. Three horse trailers were already parked along the road.

"Looks like it's going to be another beautiful day." Gramma Lisa turned off her truck's engine. "I expect we'll see more horses and bikes on the carriage roads today."

Sofia jumped from the truck to get a better look at a dark bay horse pulling a carriage with two enormous wooden wheels. The driver smiled at her, and the passenger sitting beside her waved.

"Your horse is pretty," Sofia called out.

"Thank you." The middle-aged woman halted her horse. "Her name is Bonnie. Did you want to say hello?"

Sofia approached the carriage carefully, aware that the mare's blinders prevented Bonnie from seeing her from the side. "I sometimes drive a horse, but he's a lot smaller than Bonnie. Snickers is a miniature horse."

"Ah, how fun," the passenger said. She wore a bright-pink knit hat over her braided white hair. "Bonnie is a Standardbred."

"Did she used to be a harness racing horse?"

"Yes, she retired from racing many years ago," the passenger said. "My sister and I have owned her for thirteen years. Bonny loves coming to Acadia."

Bonnie tossed her head and took a step forward.

"Stand." The driver held the fidgeting mare back.

"Are you riding today, dear?" The pink-hatted lady asked.

"Yeah. My Quarter Horse, Sundance." Sofia glanced down the road, spotting Allison's truck. "He's coming in that trailer."

"I hope you have a wonderful ride, dear," the woman said as Bonnie's driver signaled for the mare to continue their journey. "Just watch out for the bicyclists. I'm afraid they don't always respect the horses."

Sofia waved as Bonnie and the two women trotted away.

Allison seemed to be in a better mood this morning. She didn't even snap at Sofia when she was the last person to saddle and mount her horse. Thor appeared more relaxed, too. Maybe yesterday's two-hour ride had mellowed him out.

Jess explained that the day's eight-and-a-half-mile route was called Bubble Pond Loop. They'd pass Bubble Pond, Eagle Lake, and Jordan Pond, and cross over three beautiful bridges along the way. What Jess didn't say was that as they approached Bubble Pond, the road would narrow, with huge rocks bordering both sides of the path.

Sofia tightened her grip on Sundance's reins, wondering if she should fall behind Rosie instead of continuing to ride beside her. The others were walking along single file, with Thor in the lead and Magic in the rear.

Sundance's ears darted back a moment before Gramma Lisa called out, "Please be careful of the horses."

"They're too slow," a man's voice answered. "We want to pass."

Sofia shifted her shoulders to the side and craned her neck to see what was going on behind them. A red-faced, enormously fat man had dismounted from his bicycle. Beside him stood a much smaller woman dressed in spandex biking pants and a boy who looked to be about six or seven, still astride his bike.

"Gerald, please." The woman shook her head at the man before glancing at the boy. "The rules say bike riders must yield to horseback riders."

"So, we're going to be stuck behind them for the rest of the trail?" The man glared at Gramma Lisa.

"It gets wider up ahead," Jess said.

The boy circled his bike a few feet behind Magic and Gramma Lisa. If he came any closer, he'd be within kicking range. Magic didn't seem disturbed, but Gramma Lisa warned him to stay back.

Sofia's attention snapped forward as Allison whirled Thor around to face them. "Let's just canter away from these idiots. *Gerald* will probably have a heart attack if he tries to keep up with us."

"Excuse me?" The fat man shouted back.

Without waiting for the rest of the group, Allison spun her Thoroughbred back around. He bolted forward like a racehorse exploding from the starting gate—something he'd likely done many times in his past.

Caught unprepared for Sundance's sudden leap after Thor, Sofia grabbed a handful of her horse's mane to prevent herself from bouncing out of the saddle. Realizing there was little chance of stopping him now, she pushed her heels down and leaned forward into the two-point jumping position Anika had taught her. She didn't dare to look behind her, but the sound of hooves thundering over the hard-packed carriage road told her that Rosie and Magic were following behind.

The pace couldn't be described as a gentle canter, but after a few more strides, Sofia realized they weren't exactly galloping, either. It was more like a brisk, exhilarating canter. Her initial fear of Sundance racing out of control shifted into a heart-pounding thrill. Her horse was powerful and fast, and she was a capable rider. Sofia whooped as they flew down the road.

They cantered for another minute or two before Allison shouted, "Hikers ahead!" and abruptly pulled her horse into a jiggy trot.

Sundance would have careened into Thor's rear end if Sofia hadn't wrenched her reins to the left, sending him in a tight circle and nearly slamming into Rosie.

"Geez, Allison," Jess huffed. "What the heck?"

"Hikers ahead," Allison repeated. "I didn't think they'd appreciate being trampled by our horses."

"Maybe you should have thought about that before you took off without giving us any warning," Jess said.

Allison shrugged, Thor still dancing nervously under her. "You didn't have to follow."

"Give me a break," Jess snapped. "Sofia's a kid! She could have gotten hurt."

Sofia sucked in a breath, stung by Jess's comment. Sundance tossed his head, eager to continue racing up the path. "I can handle my horse," she muttered.

Gramma Lisa and Magic, who'd been lagging several hundred feet behind, finally caught up to them. "That was...unexpected," she said, frowning at Allison.

"Which part?" Jess growled. "Bolting down the trail or slamming on the brakes?"

"You've made your point," Allison shot back. "I thought it was fun. I bet Sofia did, too."

Sofia stared down at Sundance's mane. It *had* been fun. It had also been dangerous.

Gramma Lisa sighed. "Magic is huffing and puffing. He's not built for speed."

"True." Allison nodded, a smile tugging at the corners of her mouth. "Poor old Black Magic got left in the dust. But Sundance looks like he's ready for the races."

Sofia smiled despite herself. Sundance snorted and pranced, pulling against the bit.

The hikers, two silver-haired women with walking poles, waved as they approached. "Lovely morning for a ride," the shorter of the two said. "Looks like your horses are having fun."

"They are," Sofia said.

Maybe *too* much fun.

Chapter 29

Sundance continued to prance down the carriage road, eager to break free from Sofia's tight grip on the reins and overtake Thor as the leader of their expedition. Hoping it might help to settle Sundance, Sofia considered asking if they might canter again, or at least trot, but worried Jess or Gramma Lisa might interpret the request as taking Allison's side. Even worse, Jess might rebuff her as being "just a kid" who might get hurt. Gramma Lisa would certainly agree.

Thoughts of racing down the trail vanished as the road approached Bubble Pond. The path hugged the side of the tranquil water, revealing a spectacular view. The smooth humps of two mountains rose from the other side of the pond, their reflected images shimmering in the sparkling water. Gray and brown boulders poked above the surface, looking oddly out of place, as if a giant had tossed them down from the mountain and into the pond below.

The clopping sound of the horses' hooves softened as they walked over the brown pine needles and fallen leaves that coated the side of the trail closest to the pond. Bright red berries clung to a leafless shrub nestled between the tangled roots of a spruce tree.

Sofia closed her eyes and breathed deeply, taking in the damp, earthy smell of decomposing vegetation. As her anxious thoughts subsided, Sundance lowered his head and stopped straining at the bit. He blew out a long, fluttery breath and slowed his pace, allowing Thor to wander ahead while he fell in beside Rosie.

They passed a lone hiker who leaned against a huge rock as he gazed out at the pond. He didn't even look up at them as they ambled by.

They rode in silence for several minutes before Jess turned her face toward Sofia. "It's so peaceful, isn't it?"

Sofia nodded, reluctant to break the spell.

Jess leaned forward and rubbed a hand along Rosie's frosted chestnut neck. "She really likes Sundance. And I like having a riding partner." She smiled at Sofia. "We don't have a lot of good riding weather left before winter, but I hope you'll take Sundance out with me and Rosie a few more times this fall. Maybe we can convince Jason to bring Magic along, too."

"If Jason rides Magic, Olivia and Anika won't be able to come."

Jess sighed. "I'm sure it would be more fun for you to ride with them. Maybe..."

Sofia shook her head. "I don't want them to come."

"You don't?"

Sofia's cheeks flushed. "I like my friends. It's just that there's two of them and only one of Magic and they're not so great at taking turns."

"I noticed." Jess chuckled. "If it makes it easier for you, you can tell them I'm really mean and decided they aren't allowed to ride my horses."

"But they already know you aren't mean."

"Then you can blame it on Jason." She snorted. "Tell them he's caught the riding bug and simply must ride Magic every chance he gets."

Sofia smiled, imagining Jason giving up his ATV for a horse.

Allison, who was at least fifty yards ahead of the others, turned in the saddle and shouted back, "Ready for another trot?"

Sofia glanced at Jess before looking over her shoulder at Gramma Lisa.

"It's fine with me as long as she doesn't go racing off again," Gramma Lisa said.

"Sure!" Sofia called out to Allison. She brushed her legs against Sundance's sides. The palomino's pace quickened, but she needed to give him another squeeze before he broke into a smooth, unhurried trot by Rosie's side.

As she had the day before, Allison allowed Thor to pull even further ahead of the others, until the Thoroughbred eventually disappeared into the distance.

They'd been trotting for about five minutes when Sofia's phone vibrated in her coat pocket. She'd never attempted to answer her phone while riding before, but what if it was a call from Daddy? What if something terrible had happened to Daniella or Santiago? Heart racing, she took Sundance's reins into her left hand and fumbled with the zipper.

"What's wrong?" Jess asked.

"I'm getting a call." Sofia desperately tugged at the zipper, hoping the call wouldn't go to voicemail before she could answer.

Jess slowed Rosie to a walk. Sundance interpreted his friend's change in pace as a sign he should walk, too.

Sofia should have insisted he take directions from *her* instead of allowing him to make his own decisions, but she was too busy fishing the phone out of her pocket. She sucked in a quick breath when she saw Daddy's number on the screen. "Hello?"

"Hello, Sofia!" Daddy's voice sounded excited. "I've got some good news."

"Daniella is home from the hospital?" Sofia held her breath.

"No. Not yet." Daddy laughed. "She's going to stay for a few more days with your baby brother. You're officially a big sister!"

Sofia gasped. "Santiago was born? Already?"

"Yes. About an hour ago."

"Is he..." Sofia hesitated. Surely her baby brother must be healthy, or Daddy wouldn't sound so happy.

"She had the baby?" Gramma Lisa called out. "Is he okay?"

Sofia ignored her, straining to hear Daddy's voice over the sound of Magic's approaching hooves.

"He and Daniella are doing just fine. Santiago will need to stay in the hospital to be monitored for another week or so, but the doctors have assured us he's strong. Like his big sister."

Sundance flicked his ears back as Magic approached his side. "How much does he weigh?" Gramma Lisa asked.

Sofia attempted to nudge Sundance closer to Rosie in case he tried to nip at Magic. "Gramma Lisa wants to know how big he is."

"Five pounds, seven ounces," Daddy said. "I can't wait for you to meet him."

Sofia grinned. "Me, too."

"Darling, I've got to make some other calls. I'll text you some pictures soon."

Sofia let out a long breath and put the phone back in her pocket. Had God answered her prayers? Or was it just good luck that Santiago had been born safely? She decided it was best to thank God, in case he was the one responsible, but before she could, Jess called out, "Congratulations!" and Gramma Lisa demanded to know the details.

It wasn't until they were approaching Acadia's famous Jordan Pond that Sofia offered silent words of thanks.

They'd been riding for more than an hour and a half when Sofia's stomach rumbled. Breakfast seemed a long time ago, and she'd been too nervous to eat much. The news of her brother's safe, if premature, birth had dissolved the knot in her stomach, which now demanded to be filled with something edible—preferably with lots of sugar. Maybe they could stop for donuts on the way back to Sullivan Stables.

Allison had returned shortly after Daddy's call, asking if they minded if she and Thor continued ahead. She'd promised to circle back every so often to check in with them. They'd seen her only twice since, much to Sofia's relief.

"Is anyone else getting hungry?" Jess asked.

"I'm starving," Sofia admitted.

"Me, too," Gramma Lisa said. "I bet the horses are looking forward to their hay. And a nice, long drink."

"They're good sports for putting up with us." Jess gave Rosie's neck a pat. "We'll be back to Wildwood soon. Do you want to grab some lunch on the way through Bar Harbor? We've got plenty of hay in the trailer. I'm sure the horses won't mind hanging out in there for a few extra minutes while we get a sandwich."

Sofia held back a sigh. Sandwiches were better than nothing. Maybe Jason would take them out for ice cream later, assuming any ice cream places were still open in November.

Their view of Jordan Pond disappeared as the trail turned further into the woods and climbed slightly uphill. Sofia kicked her right foot out of the stirrup and flexed her ankle. She wasn't used to riding so long, and though she would never admit it, her rear end was getting sore. She stretched the other ankle and returned her feet to the stirrups. "Would you mind if we trotted again?"

"I was thinking the same thing," Jess said. She turned back to look at Gramma Lisa. "Are you up for it?"

"As long as Magic doesn't mind," Gramma Lisa said.

"I'm sure he doesn't." Sofia nudged Sundance's sides, sending him into a brisk trot beside Rosie. Gramma Lisa urged Magic forward to join them on Sundance's left side. They trotted three abreast up the winding hill.

As they rounded the next bend in the road, Sofia spotted a bay horse pulling a two-wheeled carriage. "Hey, isn't that Bonny?"

"And isn't that? Oh, no!" Gramma Lisa exclaimed as Thor and Allison appeared at the crest of the hill, racing down toward the carriage.

"She's going to spook them!" Sofia pulled back on Sundance's reins, but her unexpected jolt of adrenaline must have shot through Sundance, too. Instead of slowing down, he broke into a canter.

The carriage swerved dangerously close to the granite coping stones lining the road as Thor charged toward Bonny. Why wasn't Allison slowing her horse?

That's when Sofia spotted the pack of bicyclists coming around a bend, streaming down the hill behind Thor. Allison wasn't being reckless. Thor was running away from the bikes!

The powerful Thoroughbred streaked past Bonny and the two women in the carriage, narrowly missing the large wheels. Now they were heading straight for Sundance!

Sofia yanked Sundance to the right to avoid crashing into Thor, only to realize they were now on a head-on collision course with Bonnie.

"Whoa!" Sofia frantically pulled on Sundance's mouth, see-saw-ing the reins with all her might. He shook his head from side to side, but his pace barely slowed. If she veered to the left, Thor might crash into them, but if she continued straight, she'd only have a few seconds in which to turn before Bonny and the carriage would collide with them. And what about the bicycles?

She held her breath as Thor barreled past Sundance. Sofia didn't have time to think. She had to move out of Bonny's path now! Pulling hard on his left rein, she swerved Sundance away from the oncoming carriage.

"Mateo!" a woman's voice screeched. "Use your brakes!"

"I can't stop!" The tiny child, who couldn't have been older than six, gripped his handlebars as his bike shimmied unpredictably down the slope.

"Mateo! Watch out!" the woman shouted.

Sundance snorted and leaped sideways out of Mateo's path.

Sofia grabbed the palomino's mane, fighting to keep her balance as both of her feet flew out from the stirrups and she slipped precariously to her right. Her bottom bounced from the saddle. She clamped her left knee against Sundance's side to prevent herself from sliding to the ground. She fell forward against his neck.

"Mateo, you're going to hit the horse!"

"Eek!" The little boy cried out a split second before Sofia heard the crash.

"Lisa!" Jess shouted as a second, much louder thud reached Sofia's ears, followed by the little boy's wail. Had the boy crashed his bike into Magic?

Still clutching the reins, Sofia leaped from Sundance's back. Her knees buckled as her feet hit the ground. She nearly fell onto her rear end, but she refused to let go of the reins, and an instant later Sundance's momentum wrenched her body forward. She scrambled to her feet as Sundance circled around her and skidded to a stop.

Sofia spun around and stared in horror at the scene below. "Gramma Lisa!"

Chapter 30

Gramma Lisa lay sprawled on the hard ground. Magic stood a few feet to her left, his thick sides heaving and his reins dangling over his head. The little boy, Mateo, clutched his arm and whimpered beside his bicycle.

Sofia's heart raced as she rushed down the hill, with Sundance trotting by her side. "Gramma Lisa, are you okay?"

"I think so." Gramma Lisa sat up and groaned. "I'm going to have some bruises, though. What about the boy? Is he?"

"My bike is broken!" Mateo wailed. "The big horse smashed into me."

It was your fault, not Magic's, Sofia thought as she struggled to keep from shouting at the little boy. "Why didn't you slow down?"

"I couldn't," Mateo blubbered. "I'm sorry."

"It was an accident," Jess said, glancing down the road.

Sofia followed her gaze. The carriage driver had regained control over the frightened Bonny. Allison, now dismounted from Thor, was approaching them. Was she planning to apologize or blame the women for being in her way?

"Can you please hold Rosie for me?" Jess handed the Appaloosa's reins to Sofia and hurried to Gramma Lisa's side. "Do you think you can stand?"

Gramma Lisa took Jess's outstretched hand and winced as she struggled to her feet. "I'm going to be really sore tomorrow." She stepped closer to Mateo, who looked up at her with wide, tear-filled eyes. "That was quite the crash. Is your arm hurt?"

Mateo showed Gramma Lisa his scraped elbow while Jess examined Magic.

"Is Magic okay?" Sofia asked as Sundance and Rosie nuzzled each other. The huge gelding wasn't moving. What if the impact had broken his leg?

The other half-dozen bicyclists had dismounted and left their bikes by the side of the road. A slender, dark-haired woman approached cautiously. "Mateo, are you alright? You aren't hurt?"

The boy sniffed. "My arm hurts."

The woman shot a nervous glance at Magic and Jess before stepping closer. "What happened, Mateo? Why didn't you stop?"

"I was going too fast." He hung his head. "I was scared."

"It all happened so fast," Gramma Lisa said. "I tried to get out of his way, but there was nowhere to go."

"It wasn't your fault. We should have been more careful." The slender woman glanced down the hill. "I think we startled that horse. It suddenly took off."

Or Allison thought it would be fun to race the bike riders. Sofia narrowed her eyes at Allison and Thor as they made their way up the hill. She'd wanted to blame the bicyclists and the little boy who'd lost control of his bike, but had Allison's recklessness been the true cause of the accident? Her grip tightened on Sundance and Rosie's reins.

Gramma Lisa gazed down the road. Was she wondering the same thing?

"That was quite the scare," Allison called out. "Is everyone okay?"

"No!" Sofia shouted back. "Gramma Lisa fell off! And Mateo's bike is broken, and his elbow is hurt. And Magic..." She bit her lip.

Allison frowned. "What happened to Magic?"

Jess rubbed her forehead. "The bike slammed into him."

"Oh, no." Allison quickened her pace. "Is he injured?"

Sofia held her breath as Jess led Magic forward a few steps. Was he limping?

"Come on, boy." Jess made a kissing noise as she encouraged Magic to trot. His head bobbed up and down with each stride.

"He's definitely off in his front left side," Gramma Lisa said. "Poor guy."

"Good thing we're only a few minutes away from the trailer," Allison said. "What about you, Lisa? Do you think you can walk that far?"

"I'll do my best." Gramma Lisa ran her hand along Magic's neck. "The two of us can gimp along."

Sofia shook her head. "You should ride Sundance, and I'll lead Magic."

"Do you want me to call anyone?" the slender bike rider asked.

"We should be fine," Jess said. "Just take care of Mateo. I'm sorry about his arm. And his bike." She glared at Allison.

"Why are you looking at me like that?" Allison sounded confused and slightly hurt, but Sofia wasn't buying her *I'm innocent* act. The more she considered the possibility, the more certain she grew. Thor hadn't spooked at the bikes, at least not initially. Allison deliberately galloped away from them before losing control over her monster Thoroughbred.

Sofia studied Magic's front legs as she led him along the trail behind Sundance and Rosie. If he was in pain, he certainly wasn't showing it, but she remembered reading that because horses were prey animals, they usually hid any sign of weakness, especially in unfamiliar environments. She paused to run her hand along

Magic's left foreleg, feeling for cuts or lumps, but found none. How had the draft horse escaped serious injury? Maybe he'd leaped away from Mateo's path quickly enough to avoid the full impact of the crash, unseating Gramma Lisa in the process.

She allowed her gaze to shift to Gramma Lisa. It had taken her a long time to mount Sundance. Was she in more pain than she was letting on?

Allison should have been the one to get hurt. Not Gramma Lisa. Not Magic. If anything happened to them...

Sofia sighed. As obnoxious as Allison was, she hadn't intended to hurt anyone. Being angry with her wouldn't change what had already happened.

Although Allison hadn't accepted responsibility for the accident, at least she and Thor were no longer racing ahead of the group. She led the way at a slow walk, frequently turning in the saddle to check on the others.

They arrived at the trailer ten minutes later. No one spoke while they dismounted and untacked the horses.

Gramma Lisa limped toward the trailer's storage room with Sundance's saddle slung over one arm and his bridle tucked over her shoulder.

"Let me take care of those." Sofia hurried over to her side and snatched the saddle out of her grandmother's arms. "You should rest in your truck."

"You don't need to treat me like I'm made of glass," Gramma Lisa said. "I'm not dying, yet."

"But you're hurt," Sofia insisted. "Maybe you should go to the hospital, just in case..."

Gramma Lisa shook her head. "I'm just banged up a bit. Today wasn't the first time I've fallen off a horse and it probably won't be my last."

Sofia couldn't help glaring at Allison as she walked past with Thor's saddle. Allison pursed her lips and looked away.

Jess checked Magic's legs again before leading him into the trailer. "Magic can't be ridden tomorrow," she said after all the horses were loaded and Sofia had closed and locked the door.

Gramma Lisa nodded.

Sofia bit her lip. Of course, she'd realized that Magic couldn't be ridden, but she hadn't thought about the reality that with one fewer horse to ride, one of them would be left behind. Allison wouldn't give up the opportunity to race around the trails with Thor, and even if she did, Sofia doubted anyone else would want to ride him. Rosie belonged to Jess, and it wouldn't be fair to expect her to share her Appaloosa with Gramma Lisa.

That left Sundance.

Sofia glanced at Gramma Lisa. What would her grandmother do all day if she didn't ride with them tomorrow? Would Mom and Gramma Lisa get along, or would Mom pick a fight about something stupid that happened in their past? Maybe Gramma Lisa could hang out with Grampy. Or...

Sofia sighed. She could let Gramma Lisa ride Sundance.

Sofia and Gramma Lisa were half-way to Sullivan Stables before Sofia made up her mind. If she'd brought Anika or Olivia to Acadia, they would have expected to take turns riding Sundance if something happened to Magic. She wouldn't have wanted to share her horse, but it would have been the right thing to do.

She'd chosen to invite Gramma Lisa, instead of her friends. It wouldn't be fair to expect her to miss out on the fun. Unfortunately, Gramma Lisa would be too sore to walk or jog along, waiting for a turn on Sundance. Sofia would have to travel on foot while the others rode.

"Would you like a granola bar?" Gramma Lisa asked. "I just remembered I stashed a few in the glove compartment. I'm afraid it's going to be a while before we can grab some lunch."

Sofia opened the glove compartment and pushed aside a handful of crumpled receipts as she searched for the granola bars. "Do you want one, too?"

Gramma Lisa nodded. "I'm starving."

Sofia unearthed two packages labeled *Oats and Honey* and one marked *Sweet and Salty Nut*. Her stomach growled. She would have preferred something with chocolate in it, but at this point, she'd eat almost anything. She handed the nut-flavored one to Gramma Lisa and unwrapped the oat and honey kind, figuring that if she didn't like it, Sundance probably would.

The dry granola bar crumbled as she took a tentative bite. A chunk landed on her lap. She decided not to ask how long it had been inside Gramma Lisa's truck.

"I want you to ride Sundance tomorrow," Sofia said.

Gramma Lisa turned toward Sofia with a quizzical expression before returning her focus to the road. "Are you afraid he might run away with you again?"

"What?" Sofia shook her head. "I'm not afraid. I just thought that since you can't ride Magic, you could ride Sundance instead. I can walk beside you. Or run when you want to trot."

"Oh, sweet, dear child. You don't need to do that. I'm probably going to be too sore to ride tomorrow, anyway."

"But it's not fair to leave you behind," Sofia protested.

"Nonsense." Gramma Lisa took a bite of her granola bar. She made a face as she chewed. "Gosh, this is salty. And kind of stale." She swallowed and put the rest of the bar on her thigh. "Magic is the one I'm concerned about leaving behind. He should rest quietly. It's up to Jess, of course, but I'd worry he might get worked up and run around without a friend to keep him company."

"Not Thor, then," Sofia said.

"Goodness, no." Gramma Lisa glanced at the half-eaten granola bar on her lap, picked it up, took another bite, and grimaced. "If I were Jess, I would keep Rosie stabled next to Magic and let her crazy friend ride Thor by herself tomorrow. And I can't tell you what to do, but..."

"There's no way I'm riding with Allison." Sofia let out a slow breath. "Sundance really likes Rosie. He'd probably be a lot happier staying back with her."

"I expect so," Gramma Lisa said. "Of course, we don't know what Jess is planning."

Sofia closed her eyes. If Jess planned to ride Rosie tomorrow, someone else needed to keep Magic company. Sundance and Magic weren't best friends, but at least they knew each other. She would keep Sundance back. It was the right thing to do.

Chapter 31

Logan Sullivan was leading the gray pony, Princess, in the sandy riding ring when Sofia and Gramma Lisa pulled into the driveway. Caden waved to them from the saddle.

Though the weight over her decision not to ride tomorrow gnawed at her insides, Sofia smiled and waved back. Someday she'd give Santiago a pony ride on Sundance. They'd borrow Jess's trailer, and Jason could drive them to a horse show. She and Sundance would compete in jumping events, but the highlight of the day would be the leadline class, as she walked beside her horse with Santiago perched proudly on his back. She imagined her little brother's toothy grin as the judge handed him a blue ribbon while Daddy and Daniella cheered. Gramma Lisa would be there, too. And Grampy and Jason. But would Mom?

Her throat tightened.

Jess waited behind the trailer with Magic and Rosie's lead ropes in her hand. She glanced toward Gramma Lisa's truck.

Sofia sucked in her lower lip and unfastened her seat belt. She needed to unload Sundance instead of sitting in the truck daydreaming about events that would probably never happen.

Now familiar with the routine, Sundance calmly stepped out of the trailer, blinked a few times, and headed for a patch of grass on the edge of the driveway. Sofia allowed him to graze while Jess unloaded Rosie.

Allison and her cousin, Nicole, emerged from inside the barn, both red-faced and frowning. Had they been arguing?

"I'm sorry to hear about Magic's accident," Nicole said to Jess. "I can give our vet a call, but since it's the weekend, she might not be available. We've only been in Ellsworth for a few months, so I haven't met the other vets in the area."

Allison glared at Nicole. "Someone *must* be on call to cover emergencies."

Jess shook her head. "I don't think it's an emergency."

"Why don't we bring Rosie and Sundance to their stalls?" Nicole said. "Then we can see what's going on with Magic. And Allison?" She glared back at her cousin. "Please keep your horse under control while you lead him into the barn. We don't need any more accidents."

Sofia tugged on Sundance's lead rope, hoping to steer clear of the escalating tension between Allison, Nicole, and Jess. Her horse grabbed another mouthful of grass before raising his head.

"I'm sure you're as hungry as I am, but you can eat hay in your stall." Sundance eyed the grass again, but Sofia gave his lead a sharp yank. "Come on, buddy."

Gramma Lisa hobbled over to Jess. "I'll be happy to bring Rosie into the barn, so you can take care of Magic."

Jess nodded, and Gramma Lisa took Rosie's lead rope. Sundance craned his neck to gaze at his friend. Apparently satisfied that she would come, too, he followed Sofia into the barn.

As soon as they were out of earshot of the others, Gramma Lisa said, "Let's get the horses settled as quickly as we can and get out of here."

"What about Magic?"

"Jess and Nicole will take good care of him. There's nothing we can do except get in the way." Gramma Lisa glanced over her shoulder. "And between you and me, I do *not* want to spend another second of my day with Allison."

"Me neither," Sofia muttered as she led Sundance into his stall. She wrapped her arms around his neck, closed her eyes, and breathed in his warm, horsey scent. She stood there for another moment or two before releasing him from her embrace. "You're going to be happy here with Rosie. Just stay away from that troublemaker, Thor."

After stopping for meatball sub sandwiches in Ellsworth, Sofia and Gramma Lisa drove back to the motel in Bar Harbor. Mom, Jason, and Grampy were visiting the touristy downtown shops, but Sofia just wanted to take a nap.

"Good idea." Gramma Lisa unbuckled her seatbelt, rubbed her knee, and groaned. "I'll take a hot shower and a few ibuprofens first, though. I don't bounce as well as I used to."

Sofia's face scrunched with worry. "Are you sure you don't need to see a doctor?"

Gramma Lisa shook her head and flashed a lopsided smile. "Did anyone ever tell you that you worry too much?"

Sofia looked away, embarrassed to admit how many times Olivia, Anika, Ryan, and pretty much everyone she knew accused her of worrying too much. Still refusing to look Gramma Lisa in the eye, she hopped out of the truck, unable to ignore her grandmother's slight limp as they made their way to the motel lobby.

When they arrived in the hallway outside of Sofia's room, Gramma Lisa gave her a hug. "I'm so glad you invited me on this trip. Acadia is beautiful, and I couldn't have asked for a nicer horse to ride. But the most important thing is that I'm getting to spend time with you."

Sofia leaned against Gramma Lisa's squishy chest. Though mixed with the scents of horses and sweat, she caught a faint whiff of her lavender shampoo. "You smell nice."

Gramma Lisa's chest vibrated with her laughter. "Your mother might not agree. In fact, I suspect she'll want both of us to take a shower."

"I'll do that after I wake up." Sofia yawned and stepped away from Gramma Lisa's embrace. "Are you sure you're going to be alright?"

"What did I tell you about worrying?" Gramma Lisa chided. She glanced at her watch. "I can't believe it's almost three-thirty. Your mom wants to meet us here at five. We'd better get to work on those naps. *And showers.*"

A ping from Sofia's phone woke her an hour later. She turned over and groaned, ready to fall asleep again before realizing that the text might be from Daddy. She jumped from the bed and hurried over to the desk in the corner of the room.

Congratulations, Big Sister!

Below the text was a picture of Daddy holding a tiny baby against his chest. Santiago was wrapped in a thin blanket decorated with giraffes.

Was that a strip of tape on her brother's face?

Sofia zoomed in.

The tape secured what looked like a tiny plastic tube inserted into Santiago's nostril. Did that mean he needed help with breathing? Was her baby brother sick?

She hesitated before typing her question. She didn't want Daddy to think she was accusing him of hiding the truth about Santiago's condition—even if that was what her father had done.

He's adorable. What's the thing in his nose?

She paced around the room while she waited for a response. The weak November sun had dipped just below the horizon, casting its reddish glow against the wall.

The phone pinged again. Heart racing, she snatched it from the desk.

Nothing to worry about.

Seriously? Now her father was getting on her case about worrying, too? She let out a long breath. If there was nothing to worry about, why did her brother have a plastic tube jammed up his nose?

Ping!

Since your brother was born a few weeks early, he's still learning how to suck and swallow milk. The doctors wanted to be sure he's getting enough nutrition, so they gave him a feeding tube. It's called a Nasogastric tube. He'll only need it for a few days.

Sofia reread the text three times, trying to process what it meant. The important thing was that her brother was being taken care of and he'd only need the tube for a few days.

She studied Santiago's picture. Did he look like her? Olivia would know. Smiling, she sent the picture to Olivia.

Olivia's reply came an instant later. *OMG! Is that your brother?*

He decided he wanted to come a few weeks early. Sofia added a few emojis. *Do you think he looks like me?*

Sofia laughed at Olivia's reply. *No offence, but he's way cuter.*

Chapter 32

S ofia's thoughts were interrupted by a knock at the door. Assuming it must be Gramma Lisa, she slid her phone into her back pocket, crossed the room, and swung open the door. "Hi Gramma... Oh."

Jason grinned at her. "I hear congratulations are in order, big sister."

Sofia returned a sheepish smile, her cheeks warming at her mistake. How had he found out about Santiago?

"Is it okay if I come in?" Jason asked. "Or would you be more comfortable if we talked in the hallway?"

She stepped halfway through the open doorway and glanced down the hall. "Where's Mom?"

"She's in your grandmother's room. And Grampy is taking a nap. Your mom's marathon shopping trip tired him out." He chuckled. "Me, too, but don't tell her I said that."

Sofia smiled. Mom loved to wander around shops, even if she didn't buy anything. "You can come in."

"Thanks." Jason's face grew serious. "There's something I wanted to talk with you about. Two things, actually."

Sofia swallowed. Had Magic been more badly injured than they thought? Or even worse, what if Jason and Mom had a fight? Why else would Mom be talking to Gramma Lisa?

Jason waited for Sofia to sit cross-legged on her bed before leaning against the edge of Mom's bed. When it squeaked under his weight, he covered his mouth with his hand. "Excuse me. I knew I shouldn't have eaten that burrito for lunch."

Sofia realized Jason wanted her to laugh, but her stomach twisted so violently she feared she might vomit instead. What if Mom had broken up with Jason? Was she about to stride through the door and demand that Sofia pack her suitcase? What if she never saw Jason, or Jess, or Magic and Rosie again?

"Jess told me about what happened at Acadia today."

Sofia nodded.

"She said you were brave. And kind. She's proud of you." Jason leaned forward. "So am I."

"Thank you." Sofia stared at her clasped hands. Saying nice things to her wouldn't soften the blow that might come any minute.

Jason sighed. "She's unhappy with Allison at the moment. She thinks the accident was mostly her fault, but Allison won't take responsibility. In fact, Allison got on Jess's case and said some not so nice things that I won't repeat."

"About me?" Sofia couldn't help asking.

"No, of course not! Why would you think that?"

She shrugged.

"You are the sweetest, kindest girl in the world, Sofia. Even someone like Allison can see that." Mom's bed squeaked again as he shifted his position, but his expression remained serious this time. "Jess told me Magic is lame."

He shook his head at Sofia. "Now, don't get all worried about him. Jess assured me he's just a bit sore. After some rest, he'll be as good as new. But that means that he can't be ridden tomorrow."

"I already knew that." When was Jason going to tell her the second thing? When would he admit that he and Mom were breaking up?

"Oh." Jason scratched his chin where his scraggly beard used to be. "What you probably don't know is that Jess is going to bring Magic home tonight."

Sofia sat straighter. "What about Allison?" It was her trailer, after all.

"Allison isn't happy, but she agreed, given the circumstances, ending the trip a day early makes sense." Jason stood and leaned forward to touch Sofia's shoulder. "I'm sorry. She's taking Rosie and Sundance back, too."

Sofia unfolded her legs and hopped off the bed. She hadn't planned to ride tomorrow, but it hadn't occurred to her she'd be going home early. "Does Gramma Lisa know, yet?"

Jason nodded.

A heavy weight settled into her already churning stomach. "I'd better get my stuff packed."

"You don't need to go with them." Jason gave her shoulder a squeeze. "Please stay. Jess will take care of everything."

"But Sundance—"

"Jess wants you to stay, too. He's your horse, and we can't tell you what to do, but he's going to be just fine. He and Rosie are best buddies now, and Jess promises to deliver him safe and sound to Stephanie."

Sofia chewed on her lower lip. "What about Gramma Lisa? Is she going home?"

"Your mom and I asked her to stay, too." Jason smiled. "It's a family trip. And she's family."

If Jason was still insisting this was a *family* trip, he and Mom couldn't have broken up. So, what was the other thing he wanted to talk with her about?

"Will you please stay, Sofia?" Jason asked.

She took a deep breath before answering. "Yes."

"Great! Because I want to take you out for ice cream."

"Now? Before dinner?" Sofia studied Jason's goofy grin, searching for clues about what he was really thinking. Surely, the second thing he wanted to discuss wasn't her favorite flavor of ice cream. "And isn't it kind of cold for ice cream?"

"My motto is, eat dessert first. Plus, it's never too cold for ice cream."

Sofia laughed when Jason rubbed his hands together and bounced on the balls of his feet.

"Okay," she said, "but I haven't taken a shower yet. Mom won't like it."

"Horses!" Jason sniffed the air dramatically. "One of the loveliest aromas in the world." He raised his arm, stuck his nose into his armpit, and grimaced.

Sofia giggled. "Mom won't like that smell, either."

"Luckily for her, she's not coming with us."

"She isn't?"

"It's just you and me, kid." Jason winked. "With any luck, the other customers will flee in horror, and we'll have the place to ourselves."

They were halfway down the hallway when Sofia asked, "What's the second thing you want to talk with me about?"

Jason halted, inhaling sharply. "Uh..." He glanced out of the corner of his eye toward Gramma Lisa's room before offering Sofia a silly grin. "Going out for ice cream, of course."

She cocked her head. Why was Jason lying? If he and Mom hadn't broken up, what did he want to tell her without Mom, Grampy, or Gramma Lisa around to hear their conversation?

Jason cracked silly jokes during their short drive to Gigi's Big Scoops, refusing to reveal what he really wanted to talk with Sofia about. "Keep your eyes out for a parking spot," he said as they drove past the shop, serious for the first time since they climbed into his truck.

"I think that person is leaving." Sofia pointed at a tiny orange Honda on the opposite side of the busy downtown street.

"Looks like a clown car. Keep your fingers crossed, so no one nabs it before I can turn around."

Sofia dutifully crossed her fingers. It worked.

"Watch the master at work." Jason maneuvered his truck into the tight spot. "I'll teach you my secrets if you promise not to reveal them to your friends. They'll be in awe of your horse trailer parking skills."

"I'm only eleven. I can't drive, yet!"

Jason turned off the ignition. "You can, as long as it's on private property."

Was he being serious?

"Your first lesson will be on Monday night after supper. We'll make Jess and Grampy clean up the dishes."

"I don't know if Mom will like that."

Jason laughed. "Sooner or later, she's going to accept you're a horse girl. You'll be driving Jess's tractor by next summer. Now, let's go see if Gigi's scoops are as big as she claims."

They walked across the street, turned right, and strolled past a brightly lit bookstore and a shop window that displayed Acadia National Park sweatshirts. Sofia paused to look at a plush moose with a tiny baseball cap perched between its felt antlers.

"Do you want it?" Jason asked.

Sofia shook her head and smiled. "I was just trying to imagine Sundance wearing an Acadia hat."

"We should get him one, so he can remember this trip forever." Jason's blue eyes twinkled under the glow of the shop's window. "Come on." He reached for Sofia's hand and pulled her toward the door.

"That's silly." She planted her feet, glancing at a middle-aged couple walking up the sidewalk. When they smiled at her, she turned away, feeling her cheeks warm.

"You need a little more silliness in your life. We're getting two hats. One for Sundance, and one for you. You can be twins." When Jason gave Sofia's arm a playful tug, she followed him through the doorway and half-way down the narrow shop aisle.

Jason picked up a neon yellow baseball cap embroidered with tall pine trees and a mountain scene. "How about this one?"

Sofia wrinkled her nose. "Too bright."

He scratched his chin. "We need something that would complement Sundance's golden palomino color. If I remember correctly from my high school art class, the complimentary color for yellow is purple."

She didn't know what he was talking about, but since Sundance's halter and lead rope were also purple, she nodded. Before she had a chance to object, Jason snatched a purple Acadia hat from the display and popped it onto her head.

"It looks marvelous," he declared. "Let's buy these and get some ice cream."

Much to Sofia's relief, Jason didn't insist she wear her new Acadia hat into Gigi's Big Scoops. The middle-aged couple she'd spotted before going into the gift shop sat at a small round table. The chubby, balding man lifted his spoon in greeting.

"Your daughter is in for a treat," he said. "Gigi's has the biggest ice cream sundaes in Bar Harbor."

"I'm glad to hear this place lives up to its claim," Jason said.

Sofia glanced at Jason, surprised he hadn't corrected the man.

Jason's cheeks flushed pink. "Do you want a cone or a sundae?"

"A sundae?" Why was Jason acting so weird?

About twenty tubs of ice cream were displayed under the glass countertop, each one featuring a different flavor. Sofia searched for something with lots of chocolate in it, finally deciding on chocolate brownie with cookie crumbles. The teenager behind the counter poured a ladle of hot chocolate syrup over the ice cream, sprayed about half a can of whipped cream over that, and topped the enormous concoction with a cherry. As hungry as she was, Sofia doubted she'd be able to finish even half of the sundae.

"And you, sir?" the teenager asked.

Jason shook his head. "I'm all set."

Sofia's eyes widened. "You're not ordering ice cream?"

He shrugged.

"You can share mine," Sofia said, horrified by the prospect of Jason watching her consume the gigantic sundae by herself.

He smiled. "Thanks."

They settled at the furthest table from the middle-aged couple. The shop was otherwise empty of customers.

She stuck her spoon into the ice cream and took a bite. She swallowed and took another before pushing the bowl closer to Jason. "You need to eat some, too."

He picked up his spoon and turned it in his hands. "There's something I want to talk with you about."

Sofia let out a breath. Why was Jason so nervous? Had he been hiding the truth? Was he about to confess that he and Mom were breaking up, after all?

"I love your mother very much."

Sofia's heart hammered against her chest, waiting for the word he must be about to say. *I love your mother very much, but...*

"And I love you, too, Sofia," he said without looking up.

She squeezed her eyes closed. *No! Don't say it.*

"You and your mom and your grandfather." He took a deep breath before continuing. "It's been just me and Jess for a long time. And now we have you."

Sofia allowed herself to peek at Jason through her half-closed eyelids. He was still twirling his spoon.

"I hope you feel like we're family, too." He finally looked up. "I know I'm not your father. I don't want you to feel that I'm trying to take his place. But..."

But. He'd said the dreaded word. Yet it meant something entirely different now. Sofia's heart swelled with hope. Jason wanted to be a part of her life.

"I would like your blessing to marry your mother."

Sofia gasped.

Jason's face fell. "I know it's only been a few months. I'll understand if you aren't ready to—"

"No!" Sofia's eyes filled with tears. "I mean, yes, I want you and mom to get married.

"Really?" Jason reached for Sofia's hand, accidentally banging it with the spoon. "Oops."

"You have my blessing." Sofia jumped up from the table and flung her arms around his shoulders. "I want you to be my stepdad."

"Congratulations!" a man's booming voice called out. Sofia had forgotten about the couple at the other table. She released Jason from her bear hug and hurried back to her chair.

"Ah, thank you." Jason gave the man a grin.

Sofia leaned forward and whispered, "Does Mom know? I mean, did you ask her yet?"

"We talked about it, but I wanted to get your blessing before I made a proposal. And you know your mom. She's going to want me to do it right. Surprise her. Make it all romantic with a big, sparkly ring."

"Yeah, that's true," Sofia admitted. "So, I should keep it a secret?" How long would she have to wait before telling Olivia, Ryan, and Anika? What would she say if Gramma Lisa asked her what she and Jason had talked about?

Jason grinned. "Do you think you can hold off until tomorrow morning? Since you're not riding, I think the family needs to take a very special trip to visit Thunder Hole."

Chapter 33

Sofia twirled a lock of hair around her finger, her gaze fixated on the rear bumper of Jason's truck as it wound its way along the Park Loop Road at Acadia National Park. She caught a brief glimpse of the backs of Mom and Jason's heads before the truck disappeared around the next bend. Her stomach fluttered with nervous excitement and a twinge of apprehension.

If Mom knew of Jason's plan, she hadn't let on. Grampy had said nothing last night or at breakfast. Neither had Gramma Lisa.

"I wonder how Magic is doing," Gramma Lisa said as they passed the turnoff for Wildwood Stables.

Sofia blinked, startled by the realization she hadn't thought about Magic—or Sundance—since her visit to Gigi's Big Scoops. "I should text Jess."

Gramma Lisa shook her head. "Please don't worry about it right now. Just enjoy the lovely view. I'm sure the horses are fine. I shouldn't have brought it up."

Sofia turned the phone over in her hands, torn between Gramma Lisa's gentle request and the urge to check on the horses. Guilt washed over her like a wave crashing against the rocky shoreline. How could she have forgotten Sundance?

Because there were other pressing matters occupying her mind, she thought—like becoming a big sister, and the anticipation of

Jason's proposal to Mom. If Mom said yes, their lives would change forever. Jason would become Sofia's stepfather. Surely, they'd move from Grampy's house into Jason's place. Maybe not right away, but after the wedding? What about Sundance? It would be much too far for her bike to Stephanie's barn. Might Jess welcome Sundance into her menagerie?

Towering pines topped orange-brown cliffs that rose from the sparkling ocean. A seagull swooped over the road, its white wings glinting in the sunlight as it soared gracefully above the rocky shoreline.

Sofia inhaled deeply. She wouldn't allow guilt or worry to ruin *this* morning.

A few minutes later, Jason's right blinker flashed. Sofia clasped her hands to prevent them from shaking. They turned up a short, steep hill and pulled into a parking space next to Jason's truck. She opened her door and jumped to the pavement before Gramma Lisa had switched off the engine.

Sofia danced from foot to foot and rubbed her arms as the brisk, salty breeze tickled her cheeks.

Jason grinned at her from inside his truck. Was he as nervous as she was? He opened his door and bounced out of the truck like there were springs on the bottom of his sneakers.

It took Sofia a moment to realize he was mirroring her movements. She planted her feet on the asphalt and crossed her arms over her chest. "Are you making fun of me?"

"Why would I do that?" He winked. "Can you please help your Grampy while I open the door for your beautiful mother?"

"I don't need help." Grampy humphed as he slid from the back seat. "I'm not a feeble old man."

"Of course not, Mr. Richardson," Jason said before jogging to the other side of the truck to open Mom's door.

"What are you doing, Jason?"

Sofia couldn't see what he was doing, but Mom giggled.

"Put me down," she demanded, though her tone sounded amused rather than annoyed.

"Not unless you give me a kiss," he said.

Sofia covered her face with her hands, glad she couldn't see them. She desperately wanted Mom to say yes to Jason's marriage proposal, but the thought of them kissing in front of her made her shiver with disgust.

Gramma Lisa joined Sofia and Grampy. "Burr." She zipped up her coat. "Aren't you cold in just your sweatshirt, Sofia? Maybe you should get your jacket."

A gush of wind sent a discarded paper coffee cup tumbling across the parking lot.

"I'm fine." Sofia held back a shiver, wishing Gramma Lisa hadn't mentioned the jacket. If she got it from the truck now, everyone would think she was a little kid who needed to be reminded about basic things like wearing jackets when it was cold outside.

Jason wrapped his arm around Mom's waist and pulled her closer. "I can't wait to show you Thunder Hole."

He led the way down the short hill and across the road to a wide stairway with metal rails on either side. Three beautiful blonde women, dressed in identical puffy blue coats with matching knit hats and mittens, gazed out at the rocky shoreline.

"Excuse me." The tallest of the women held out her phone. "Could one of you please take our picture?" Her accent sounded like English wasn't her first language.

"Sure," Jason said, letting go of Mom's hand to take the lady's phone. "Where are you from?"

"Sweden." The woman smiled and nudged one of her companions, who responded in what must have been Swedish. All three laughed.

Mom rolled her eyes.

Jason took several pictures while the women posed like they were models in a fashion shoot. For all Sofia knew, they *were* models. She glanced at Mom, wishing she could tell her not to be jealous of these silly women.

Mom cleared her throat.

Jason smirked at Mom before handing the phone back to the woman. "Would you take a picture of our family?"

"Of course," she said.

Our family. Warmth spread through Sofia's chest. *But only if Mom says yes.* Sofia pressed closer to Mom. She *had* to say yes.

Jason fumbled through his coat pocket, frowning.

"You can use my phone," Sofia offered.

He shook his head. Was it her imagination, or had Jason's face blanched white?

Mom tapped the front pocket of his jeans and laughed. "Your phone is right here."

"Oh, yeah." Jason bit his lip.

Why was he acting so weird?

Jason gave his phone to one of the three blonde women—she was too confused by Jason's sudden mood shift to notice which one—and glanced nervously at Sofia.

Grampy put one arm around Sofia's shoulder and the other around Gramma Lisa's. Mom fluffed her hair and leaned her head against Jason.

"Say cheese," the woman said. The others laughed like she'd told a hilarious joke.

Sofia forced a smile.

The woman handed the phone back to Jason. "Do you like it?"

Mom snatched it out of his hand and studied the photo. "It's okay, I guess."

"I could take another if you want," the woman replied.

Jason shook his head. "We're all set. Thanks." Then he turned to Sofia. "Could I speak with you for a second? In private?"

Mom quirked an eyebrow, but said nothing.

"What?" Sofia asked once they were out of earshot of the others. What if Jason had changed his mind about proposing to Mom?

He leaned down and whispered into her ear. "I'm sure I put the ring in my pocket, but it's not there now. I checked before I got out of the truck, so it must be somewhere between here and the parking lot."

Sofia swallowed and glanced back toward Mom, who was posing for a picture with Gramma Lisa. "What are you going to do?"

"If I search for it, she's going to ask what I'm doing. If I tell her, it will ruin the surprise." Jason looked at the three women, who were slowly making their way back toward the road. "I'm afraid someone might find it and…"

"Do you want me to look for it? I could say…" Sofia hesitated, trying to come up with a good excuse. "I could say that I'm too cold and I need to get my jacket."

"Would you do that for me?"

"Of course." Sofia sucked in a breath. "Tell Mom I'm getting my jacket."

Without waiting for his reply, she started back up the path, scanning the ground as she went. She hurried past the Swedish women, ignoring their greetings, and crossed the Park Loop Road.

Her heart pounded. The ring could be anywhere. What if someone had already found and stolen it? What if a car had crushed it under its tires? What if it had blown away in the wind?

Focus.

She needed to retrace their steps. Slowing her pace, she zigzagged up the hill leading to the parking area.

No ring.

She turned to the left, studying the pavement with each step.

No ring.

She spotted the discarded coffee cup crushed under the rear wheel of a white SUV. A middle-aged man sat in the driver's seat, staring at his phone while his German Shepherd lunged and barked at her from behind the window.

Ignoring the dog, she peered under the vehicle.

No ring.

She arrived at Gramma Lisa's truck. If the ring had fallen out of Jason's pocket, could it have rolled underneath one of the trucks? She got down on her hands and knees.

"Did you lose something?" The sound of the woman's accented voice startled Sofia.

She considered telling the woman she hadn't, but why else would she be crawling around the pavement? Maybe the Swedish women could help her. She looked up. "A ring."

The woman bent down. "You lost your ring? What does it look like?"

"I'm not sure." Sofia sucked in a breath. "It's an engagement ring. Jason, that guy who took your picture? He's going to give it to my mom, only it fell out of his pocket."

"Oh, my! He's going to propose to her?" She looked at her two friends and said something to them in Swedish. They covered their mouths. "We must help you find it."

The tall woman spoke several more words in Swedish, and the three of them fanned out along the parking lot, scanning the ground and peeping under the few cars parked there. Sofia searched the area on both sides of Gramma Lisa's truck. If she didn't find it soon, Mom would know something was wrong. She might even suspect something now, since Jason had taken Sofia aside before she suddenly needed to retrieve her jacket from the truck.

Next, she searched beside Jason's driver's side door. He'd been sure it was in his pocket before he got out of his truck, but maybe it had slipped from his pocket when he'd jumped out.

No ring.

A bead of sweat trickled down her forehead. She stood and carefully examined the pavement as she made her way to the other side of the truck. Jason had lifted Mom from her seat and insisted she kiss him before he set her down. Had the ring fallen out while she was squirming to get away? Sofia's pulse pounded in her ears as she studied the ground.

No ring.

Her eyes prickled. Without a ring, Jason couldn't propose to Mom. And if he didn't propose…

Something shiny glinted from the scruffy grass at the edge of the curb.

"Yes!" Sofia rushed forward and snatched the diamond ring from the dirt. She cupped it in her right hand and blew away the gritty dust.

One of the ladies shouted a string of nonsensical syllables and jogged over to Sofia. "Ja?" She pointed to Sofia's hand.

Sofia nodded and opened her palm to show her the ring.

The woman shouted to the others. Then she embraced Sofia and murmured something Sofia couldn't understand. The two others surrounded her, chattering excitedly.

"You found it!" the tallest woman exclaimed. "You are a hero!"

Sofia's cheeks flushed. "I have to go."

She was halfway down the hill when she realized she hadn't remembered to get her sweatshirt. Exhaling sharply, she hurried back to Gramma Lisa's truck, careful not to drop the ring. With luck, Mom wouldn't notice anything suspicious.

Except for the three Swedish women.

Giggling, they followed Sofia back down the hill and across the street. She looked over her shoulder and shook her head at them, but they didn't understand. Or, maybe they had, but decided the show was much too exciting to miss.

Sofia sighed. She'd found the ring. Jason's plan hadn't been ruined. That was all that mattered.

Chapter 34

Although she was tempted to race down the steps and thrust the ring into Jason's hand, Sofia realized this might tip Mom off to Jason's plan. She gripped the metal railing, inhaled a deep breath of the salty air, and counted to three before heading down the stairs.

Grampy, Gramma Lisa, and Mom leaned against the railing that surrounded the lowest platform, oblivious to Jason's plan as they gazed at the chasm below. A wave crashed against the rocks, shooting foaming spray into the air.

Jason looked up at Sofia, his eyes wide and pleading. When she nodded solemnly and tapped her jacket pocket, he grinned and gave her a thumbs up. If he wasn't careful, Mom would catch him acting strangely and wonder what he and Sofia were up to. Of course, Jason flashed her goofy grins all the time, so Mom might think nothing of it.

The three Swedish women would be a different story. They laughed and nudged each other as they followed Sofia down the stairs. One even held her phone out. What was she planning to do? Post Jason's marriage proposal to social media?

Sofia gritted her teeth. She'd found the ring without their help. They had no business butting in on her family's private business.

"Warm enough now?" Jason asked when Sofia joined him beside the railing.

"Yeah, thanks." She inched closer to Jason and reached into her pocket.

Mom looked up, narrowing her eyes at the women who stood on the platform above them. "Why are they staring at us?"

Jason shrugged. "They're probably just getting a better look at Thunder Hole."

"But they were already here." Mom glared at them.

Sofia turned her focus to the damp concrete under her feet, afraid of what the women might do or say if she caught their gaze.

"Hey, Sofia," Jason said as he brushed his hand against Sofia's. "Watch what happens when this wave rushes in between the gap in the rocks."

It took all of her willpower to look down at the water instead of watching Jason's hand as he stealthily reached into her jacket pocket.

The wave streamed into the narrow channel between the rocks and entered a small cavern. The sea water gurgled, and then, with a thunderous whoosh, shot back out through the hole. It splashed high in the air, spraying Sofia's face with salty froth.

"Good thing you got your jacket," Jason said as the foaming water was sucked back down the channel toward the churning ocean. He smiled at her as he slid the diamond ring into his own pocket. "My dad took Jess and me here one October after a big storm. The waves were so wild you would have been swept into the ocean if you stood where we're standing now."

"Those women are still staring at us," Mom muttered under her breath.

"They are," Gramma Lisa said, sounding as annoyed as Mom. "I'm going up there to ask them what their problem is."

"Please don't," Sofia pleaded.

Gramma Lisa crossed her arms over her chest. "They're being rude."

If Jason didn't act soon, Mom and Gramma Lisa would pick a fight with the silly women. It would ruin everything. Sofia nudged his hand and took a few steps backward, hoping he'd take the hint. Another wave whooshed from the cavern, spraying them with mist.

"Um, Mandi?" Jason took an unsteady breath.

"What?" Mom still glared at the women.

"Mandi," he repeated, reaching for her hand and giving it a gentle tug.

When Mom finally turned to him, he dropped onto one knee.

Gramma Lisa gasped.

Mom's eyes widened. "What are you?" She covered her mouth. "I thought..."

Sofia held her breath, barely noticing Grampy's hand on her shoulder.

"Mandi Richardson, I love you."

Whoosh! Spray frosted Jason's hair.

"Would you please marry me?" With his free hand, he offered the ring to Mom.

Mom stared at it, her mouth hanging slightly open. "It's beautiful, Jason." She took a shaky breath and turned her gaze to Sofia.

Sofia bounced on the balls of her feet and nodded encouragingly. "Say yes, Mom!"

Mom smiled back and offered her left hand to Jason. "Yes."

The Swedish ladies clapped as Jason slipped the ring onto Mom's finger. Mom raised an eyebrow. "They knew?"

Jason winked at Sofia. "I think you'll have to ask your daughter about them." Then, before Mom could say anything else, he stood and swept her into a passionate embrace.

Embarrassment flushed Sofia's cheeks. She squeezed her eyes closed, only to open them again a moment later to peek between her fingers. Warmth bubbled up from deep inside her and a smile spread across her face. Mom was happy. Jason was happy. And she was happy.

Grampy pulled Sofia into a tight hug. She closed her eyes again, feeling the steady thud of his heartbeat as she was enveloped in the warmth of his presence. In that moment, with the sound of the waves crashing against the rocks, she knew exactly where she belonged. This was her family. Grampy. Gramma Lisa. Mom and Jason. Even Jess.

As Sofia reveled in the warmth of the moment, her thoughts drifted to the unknown future that lay ahead. She was a big sister now. In just a few weeks, her father would wrap his arms around her for the first time in years. She'd meet Daniella and Santiago, Abuela, and the aunts and uncles and cousins she'd only recently learned she'd had. The prospect filled her with a mix of excitement and anxiety.

But as she stood there, cradled in Grampy's arms, peace washed over her. Whatever challenges awaited her, she wasn't alone.

Sofia guided Sundance in a less-than-round circle as they cantered around Snickers and Kit Kat's paddock. It was difficult to concentrate with Anika and Olivia barking conflicting orders at her while Ryan followed Anika around like a lovesick puppy.

"Push your heels down!" Olivia commanded.

"Relax. Breathe, Sofia." Anika flipped her sleek black hair over her shoulder and grinned at Ryan, apparently sharing a private joke with him.

Sofia obediently sucked in a deep lungful of air, though how Anika knew she'd been holding her breath remained one of the many mysteries of her friend's coaching abilities. Of course, Anika would be a much more effective teacher if she focused her full attention on Sofia and Sundance, rather than shamelessly flirting with Ryan for half of her lesson.

"Eyes up!" Olivia shouted. "Look toward the jump."

Sofia tore her gaze from her silly friends and focused on the low vertical. Anika had set it at two feet—barely a hop for her talented horse—but they were only warming up, and Sofia didn't want to push him too hard after their adventure in Acadia two days earlier.

The jump was three canter strides ahead. Sofia pushed her heels down—Olivia was always right, of course—and lifted her weight forward and out of the saddle. She relaxed her elbows, stretched her hands forward on his neck, and grabbed a handful of mane. She wanted to give Sundance plenty of room to propel himself over the jump without accidentally pulling back on his mouth if she fell behind the motion.

As Sundance lowered his head and gathered his powerful hindquarters, a quiver of excitement fluttered through Sofia's stomach. Then they were lifting off. Soaring. Flying!

"Very nice," Anika said.

Ryan tugged at the sleeve of her jacket. "When will you teach me how to jump?"

Olivia snorted. "Like never?"

"You'll need to practice a few other skills first," Anika said.

"After I learn how to trot and canter?" Ryan asked hopefully.

Sofia sighed. They needed more horses, but that was a problem for another day. "I have something to tell you guys."

"About Santiago?" Olivia asked.

"Something else." Sofia had texted the photo of Daddy holding her tiny brother to all three of them, but she wanted to share the news of Mom and Jason's engagement in person. She'd been tempted to call Olivia while they drove home from Acadia last night, but Olivia would have told Ryan and Ryan would have told Anika, and that would have spoiled the excitement of seeing their reaction.

Sofia dismounted and led Sundance into the middle of the makeshift riding ring. "I'm going to be moving again."

"No." Ryan stepped back and shook his head.

Olivia's shoulders drooped and her face fell. "You can't move away."

"What are you going to do with Sundance?" Anika wrapped her arms around herself and made a whimpering noise.

Sofia turned away from her friends as she attempted to hide her grin. She rubbed her hand along Sundance's furry neck, touched by their reactions.

"Did..." Olivia hesitated. "Did your mom...?"

A bubble of amusement tickled Sofia's belly. Her face contorted with the effort of holding it down, and her body shook. Then she threw her head back as the laughter burst from her mouth in a joyful explosion. "She's getting married! Jason proposed to her yesterday!"

Sundance snorted at the sound of Olivia's high-pitched screech.

"That's awesome," Anika said. "Congratulations."

"You're moving to his house?" Ryan asked.

"Not yet. We're waiting until after Christmas. After I get back from visiting Santiago and my dad and his family." She hesitated, smiling to herself. "I mean, *my* family. My other family."

"I'm so happy for you," Olivia said. "So, you're going to keep Sundance at Jess's place?"

Sofia nodded. "I haven't told Stephanie or Grace, so please don't say anything yet. I'm really going to miss seeing Snickers and Kit Kat every day, though."

"You'll still see them during our Mini Whinnies meetings," Olivia said. "Just because Sundance won't be here doesn't mean we're going to stop coming. Grace promised to take us to another show next summer."

"You and Olivia can share Snickers, and Anika and I will work with Kit Kat together," Ryan said. "And we can ride Sundance, Magic, and Rosie at Jess's house."

Olivia elbowed her brother in the ribs. "Who made you the boss?"

"Ow!" He jumped back, glowering at Olivia. "What? You're afraid I'm going to steal *your* job?"

Olivia stuck out her tongue. "I'm not bossy. I just have good leadership skills."

Anika smirked.

Sofia shook her head, laughing.

"Okay, okay." Olivia rolled her eyes. "Maybe I'm a little bossy...sometimes."

With a smile playing at the corners of her lips, Sofia turned back to Sundance. Her friends knew what they wanted, but so did she. She could stand up to them and make her own choices, no matter how difficult they may be. Whatever challenges awaited her, Sofia was ready to face them head-on, with her friends by her side and her family—both old and new—in her heart.

While the characters and most of the settings in *Sofia's Choice* live only in my imagination and on the pages of this book, Acadia National Park is real. My grandparents lived in a small town about twenty miles from Acadia. I visited the park many times as a child and have returned frequently as an adult. I have fond memories of climbing the Beehive and Mount Dorr, wandering around the grounds of Jordan Pond House, walking and biking along the carriage trails, and visiting Thunder Hole.

As a child, I dreamed of riding horses along the trails, but didn't get the opportunity until I was in my twenties. A friend invited me to accompany her and her Morgan gelding, High Note (a horse I had owned as a teenager), and I brought Cheval, an Arabian/Quarter Horse mare. We stabled the horses at Wildwood Stables and spent the next three days exploring the park on horseback.

High Note and Cheval were fast and full of energy. On our first ride, we completed the 8.5-mile Bubble Pond Loop (the same route Sofia took on her second ride) in about an hour, a pace Allison and Thor would have appreciated. On the last day of our trip, we took a more leisurely ride up Day Mountain.

Twenty-seven years later (in 2021), I rode up Day Mountain a second time, on a 26-year-old Standardbred mare named Soprano. It was a warm October day, with lots of sun, beautiful foliage, and breathtaking views of the ocean. We did some trotting, but certainly didn't set the trails on fire with our speed.

My riding partner was my instructor, fellow horse-book author, and friend, Robyn Cuffey. In addition to rescuing and retraining Standardbred racehorses, Robyn loved to ride and drive her horses along Acadia's carriage trails. She organized several trips each year. These trips filled up quickly, and most participants brought their own horses, so I was thrilled when a spot opened up for me to join her and borrow Soprano for the day.

Despite a diagnosis of pancreatic cancer in 2023, Robyn continued to show her rescued Arabian gelding at the third level in dressage and made several trips with her horses to Acadia, the last only a few weeks before her death. She was an amazing horsewoman and an inspiration to all who were blessed to have known her.

If you'd like to visit Acadia National Park on horseback, I recommend Robyn Cuffey's book, *Equestrians' Guide to Acadia*, which you can purchase from her sister, Carol, at robyncuffeybooks@gmail.com.

For pictures and video of my horseback trips to Acadia, check out my website: https://lauraholthaslam.com/visiting-acadia-national-park-on-horseback/

Are you curious about Sundance's life before he met Sofia? Check out *Sundance*, a standalone novella.

Some losses leave you without words. Sometimes, kindness helps you find your voice.

Twelve-year-old Malachi often feels isolated. His stutter makes words hard to form and friendships hard to begin, leaving him most at ease with his loyal dog, Sunny—who understands him without words. When Sunny is gone, Mal is left alone with a grief he doesn't know how to express.

Overwhelmed with sorrow, Mal wanders alone, unsure where he's headed. Hearing a horse's whinnies nearby, he follows the sound to a pasture, where he discovers a pregnant mare confined without food or water. Convinced Sunny has somehow led him to her, Mal commits to keeping the horse safe until her foal is born.

When Mal trusts a classmate with his secret, he takes a risk that feels far more dangerous than speaking out loud. But as a cautious friendship begins to grow, caring for the mare and her newborn foal helps Mal find the courage to speak up when it matters and stand firm for what he knows is right.

Sundance is a tender middle-grade novella about grief, friendship, and finding your voice—even when words don't come easily.

Find *Sundance* at your favorite online retailer:

https://books2read.com/sundance/

About the Author

Multi-award-winning author and lifelong horse enthusiast, Laura Holt-Haslam, writes uplifting novels for tweens and horse lovers of all ages, inspiring them to be more courageous, compassionate, and resilient. While horses play an important role in her stories, the heart of her writing revolves around themes of friendship, family, and the healing power of love and forgiveness. Her stories feature relatable, diverse characters who model integrity as they work hard to overcome challenges and achieve their dreams.

Laura is the mother of two young adult children. She lives in Southern Maine with her husband and two adorably naughty cats. She and her daughter share ownership of Max, a palomino miniature horse who loves to jump.

Learn more about Laura and her books, and Max and his friends at https://lauraholthaslam.com/.

Also by Laura Holt-Haslam

Standalone novella
Sundance

Sofia's Story
Sofia's Surprise
A Place for Sofia
Sofia and Sundance
Sofia's Choice

Emily Edwards Equestrian Extraordinaire
Emily Edwards Equestrian Extraordinaire
Emily Edwards to the Rescue

Guided Journals
Grateful: A Guided Gratitude Journal for Young Horse Lovers
Pawsitively Grateful: A Guided Gratitude Journal for Young Dog Lovers
Purrfectly Grateful: A Guided Gratitude Journal for Young Cat Lovers